Tell Nikki Urban what you think about the book!!!

Call Nikki Urban and tell her your comments!!!

904. 469.6353

Also By Nikki Urban:

DAMAGED GOODS

DiamondStone Productions
PO Box 11266
Jacksonville, FL 32239-11266
Printed in the United States of America
ISBN-13: 978-0615497402
ISBN-10: 0615497403

Thanks

I want to thank God for his blessings that He has bestowed upon me.

To my husband, I thank you for all of your Love, dedication and support. To my mother and father Thank you for your Love and support in making my dreams come true!

To my god-father thank you for everything- I love you so much!

To my little sisters- The both of you are my heart and I love the two of you so much!

To the Click!!!!! I love you all of you like you are my sisters!

To Gerry your skills are amazing! I look forward to working with you again on the next book's cover!

To Chanel for your Vision for the cover!

Last but not least- to the fans of Jade's Diary. Without you this book could not have been a success. All my gratitude and love is for you.

"Mikleah your mother wanted you to have this." Jaylyn said to her niece.

As she looked at her aunt with tears in her eyes, she asked her, "What has my mother left me?"

Her aunt led her to her bedroom and they sat on the bed. She held Mikleah in her arms and said, "Your mother loved you so much. She had many secrets. We never questioned or judged your mother. We loved Jade unconditionally. A year ago she gave me this diary and told me, once she was gone to give it to you. What's inside the diary I don't know. I never asked and I never read the diary." She replied.

With more questions than answers, Mikleah kissed her aunt and took the book into her hands. She wondered what her mother wanted her to know —only time would tell.

It had been a month since her mother's death and Mikleah missed her. There were so many things she needed to tell her... so many things she was afraid to tell her.

As her thoughts wondered back to her childhood, her cell phone rang. Mikleah smiled as she answered because her girl was on the phone.

"What's up baby!" She said as she spoke in the receiver of the phone.

5

"Hey Kleah, I was thinking about you. I wanted to know if you wanted company." She asked.

Kleah looked at the clock and it read 7:00 p.m. "Yeah, Rosslyn. I do want you to come over here and get some of this lovin. Give me about an hour before you come." Mikleah said. "Ok, Kleah. I'll see you in a while." Ross said as the phone went dead.

As soon as she hung up the phone, Mikleah undressed and looked at herself in the full-length mirror. The reflection showed a 20- year old, 5'5, 125 pound, coca brown woman with hazel eyes. Yes, she had broken a few hearts along the way, but it was never done intentionally. She was looking for what she needed and right now; what Mikleah needed was pussy.

As soon as she showered and toweled off, the doorbell rang. She went to the door butt ass naked and opened it. When the door opened she pulled Ross inside and began to kiss her while leading her to the bedroom.

They fell on the bed and Kleah's hands wondered over Ross' body. Her mouth went to her nipples and her hands went to her pussy. She opened her pussy lips and started to massage her clit with her thumb. Mikleah placed her fingers in her moist walls. She could feel Ross' juices warming up like she was about to explode.

6

Mikleah got up and placed her wet pussy in Ross' face. Her clit rode Ross' tongue. Before she was about cum in her mouth she jumped off her tongue and maneuvered her body on top of hers in the 69 position. They both ate until they were satisfied, but Mikleah was not done with her. She went over to the dresser and got her 8-inch strap-on dildo.

After putting on the dildo she went back to the bed and placed her head back in her pussy. She turned her over, grabbed her ass from behind, and fucked her from the back. She entered Ross slow and steady.

She was beating it from the back and playing with her clit at the same time. Ross was so turned on that she was throwing it back to Kleah. Ross came back on the dildo and exploded. Ross was shaking and didn't want the dildo out of her... she wanted to enjoy her orgasm.

Afterwards Mikleah held Ross in her arms as she slept. Mikleah got up and went to the bathroom to wash. While she was in the bathroom she began to think about her mother's diary. She finished in the bathroom, went to her purse, grabbed the book, and went back to the bed to begin reading her mother's diary.

The Jump Off
Chapter 1

November 15, 1985-Entry 1

As, I sit here on my couch with my hand massaging my clit, my other hand grabbing my tit; my thoughts went to the one who I wanted- needed to be fucking; instead of me fucking myself.

I masturbated until I trembled in ecstasy. I just sat there with my hand in my juices enjoying my touch-debating if I wanted to bust one more time before work.

Instead, I got up, went to the bathroom, and turned on the shower. As the water ran down my body, I wondered to myself: How did I get involved with the woman whose husband I had been having an affair with? But, from the first time I saw her, I knew I would be fucking Roses. One look at Roses and my pussy was instantly wet with desire for her.

When I first saw Michael, I was mesmerized by how handsome he was. He was 6'2, 230 pounds of solid muscle, with a smooth dark chocolate complexion, and hazel eyes. Michael is the FedEx deliveryman who comes to the office everyday at 3 pm with packages. As the owner of my own marketing firm, Enterprise Marketing, I pass him daily coming from my afternoon meetings.

At first, I was just flirting with him. It was just harmless bumping into him and getting a feel of his goods. The flirting led to daily phone calls. Finally, I told him I wanted what I wanted- him.

Michael told me about his home situation. He told me that he had never stepped out on his wife Roses. But, like I told him, you have already stepped out on your wife. He could not deny that he was in a you, me, and he dilemma.

The first time we consummated our affair, I remember it like it was yesterday.

"Jade, you know I will have a hard time getting away from Roses tonight. Especially, after I told her that I would be home by at least by 6:00." Michael stated in our earlier phone conversation.

As I typed away responding to a letter from a client, I thought about what he said. I called him back as I fantasized about us fucking for the first time. I wanted this more than ever and I was going to say whatever it took to get Michael to see things my way.

As soon as Michael answered the phone, I spoke before he could say hello.

"Look, Michael I don't have time for the high

school games! If you want to make this happen between us, then you make it your business to get out of the house! I don't care about what you told your wife! If you want this pussy, you know where I will be. IF I DON'T SEE YOU HERE AT MY OFFICE BY EIGHT, THEN LET'S END IT HERE!" I told him.

I figured playing the hard road would be the way to go since Michael was a man who thought with his dick rather than his head. I knew he would be in my office before eight.

I completed the finishing touches of my workload, and walked out of my office to make sure that everyone else was gone for the day. I went back to my office and closed the door. While awaiting Michael's arrival, I opened the armoire that held the 30-inch television with the VCR. I played a porn tape of two black girls in the 69 position. As I watched them going down on each other, I began fantasizing about my wet pussy lips wrapped around the tongue of the mocha brown one.

I never considered myself to be a lesbian, but I do love being with women, as well as being with men. However, I was always very choosy about whom I let go down on me; or who I went down on.

As I was fantasizing about having my pussy eaten,

out of the corner of my eye, I saw Michael coming through my door.

It was as if we could read each other's mind, because we instantly tore each other's clothes off. He threw me on the desk and began sucking my erect nipples. I moaned from the intense pleasure he was giving me with his mouth.

As he sucked my nipples, his fingers found their way into my pussy juices. He massaged my clit and then ventured down to taste me. He blessed me until I exploded in his mouth. Not wanting him to stop pleasuring me with his tongue, I placed my hand on his head and pushed my clit further into his mouth. I rode his tongue until I was about cum again.

I pushed him to the floor and took his thick dick in my hand. I pushed his manhood inside my pussy. He felt so good in me that I had to control myself before I collapsed in rapture all over his dick. I mounted the tip of his dick, gripped it with my pussy walls, and slowly came down. I began to ride him like he was my black stallion.

I can still hear him moaning and begging me not to stop. Just before he came, I jumped off him, and sucked his dick until he exploded in my mouth. When we were finished we laid on the floor not saying a word.

I got up to get dressed and Michael came behind me. He grabbed me by the waist and whispered in my ear, "You will be my lady. The only other woman I will see besides my wife. You know the rules to the game and as long as you are willing to abide by them we can be together." He said.

I turned, looked into his eyes, and nodded my head. I had already made up my mind before we fucked; that I would be his woman on the side. His dick sealed the deal.

April 5, 1986-Entry 2

Six months into our illicit love affair, it was now time for us to take our relationship to the next level of intimacy. I was seeing Michael everyday at work and we were fucking at least three to four times a week. I never had a problem with sharing him with his wife. I just wanted to be with him when I wanted, and I wanted him with me until the sun crept through my windowpane.

It was now April and we had been kicking it since November. Part of my New Year's resolution was to get Michael to start spending the night with me. I understood and accepted that I would never be able to spend the holidays with him because of his obligations. I was never the one to start drama, because once it was started, I had to finish it.

In mid January, I began to plant the seed in Michael's head that he needed to be in my bed at night and not in his wife's bed. I knew that it was going to take some convincing, but I was going to have my way. I just needed to approach the situation in a non-confrontational way.

I began to but my plan into action. I started by doing the oldest trick in the book, divide and conquer. I had to cause confusion between Michael and his wife. I started by tapping into his cell phone while he was in the shower at my house and retrieved his home, wife's cell and work numbers. I stored the numbers in my mental rolodex.

I was going to see how deep his wife's love was for her husband. I wanted to see how much of his shit she was willing to take; before she came looking for the other woman who was fucking her husband.

One thing I know from experience; whenever there is another woman involved, the main woman always wants to see her competition. I don't care how long a woman has been with her man or how good he may be to her; if her man is sticking his dick in some other woman's pussy, she wanted, better yet, she needed to know with whom.

Although, I enjoyed not being bothered with the bullshit of a relationship, I was becoming attached to

Michael in the sense that I was feeling him and what he was giving me. The feelings that I have for Michael, was my motivation to get him away from his wife, and into my life fulltime.

I do admit, I have never really given a fuck about the people who I have fucked, but it was something about Mike that just wouldn't let me put up my guard. I didn't want to break up his happy home. I just wanted more of him than I already had.

I was going to shake up his happy home with preempted attacks. I was just going to keep his wife's info handy. When it was time for me to use those numbers, I would be ready. Until then, I was just going to keep it movin.

April 15, 1986…Entry 2-cont…

I knew I had to act fast in getting my situation turned around with Mike. The first thing I did was hire a private investigator to look into Roses' background. I wanted to know everything about her; down to the color underwear she wore.

Once the investigation was complete, I would be able to enact phase two of my plan. In the meantime, I was going to give his wife a reason to doubt her so-called faithful husband.

I knew that on the days Michael was not with me he was coaching pee wee football at Hill Park. I decided I would surprise my man and watch him practice, but not without inviting his wife to come watch too. It was time to call Roses. I went to the pay-phone three blocks from the park and called her at home.

I remember the conversation plain as day……
"Hello, is Ms. Jenks home"? I asked waiting for her to respond. "Yes, this is she. Who's calling?" She said questioning the unfamiliar voice on the other end of the receiver.

"It really doesn't matter who I am. Just think of me as a concerned citizen; who wanted to tell you that you might want to keep better tabs on your husband!" I said as my response.

"Who is this playing on the damn phone and what the hell are you talking about?" Roses asked.

"Like I said before, your husband has a wandering eye. You might want to check that, especially since he has access to all of his player's mothers, who will do anything to be in his bed." With that bug in her ear, I hung up the phone and walked away from the pay-phone with a smile on my face.

I walked the three blocks to the park for my surprise visit. I walked onto the field with my head held high. I looked good enough to eat; with my tight fitting jeans, white wife beater, and my six inch Nine West pumps.

As I approached, I could see the shock in Mike's eyes. I knew he wasn't ready to see me out in public. I walked up to him, grabbed his hand, and kissed his cheek. I stood next to him like I knew he was my man. I stood there waiting for his wife to magically appear.

As I watched his team practice, I saw from the distance a beautiful woman walking towards us. She was flawless. Right then I knew she was his wife. She was 5'5, 120 pounds, and had a bob haircut. She was shaped like a coke bottle with a "D" sized chest. As I watched her approach us, I fantasized about turning her out. Just by looking at her, I knew her pussy would be good.

Mike didn't realize she was coming. When he looked up from calling the play, he had the look of terror on his face; like a deer caught in headlights. Seeing the look in his eyes made me laugh to myself. I could tell he thought he was caught out there without a ladder to pull himself out of the storm. Being who I am, this is how I wanted it to go down...with me to save his ass from disaster.

I began to walk toward her as she got closer. When I was close enough I started a conversation.

"Hello, are you one of the boy's mother's?" I asked her already knowing the answer. She looked at me, smiled, and said, "No, I'm coach Jenks' wife."

"Oh, ok, well my name is Jade. My nephew is on his team. I was supposed to pick him up, but I think my sister and I got our signals crossed. She called coach Jenks and told him that she would be picking him up and I didn't need to come. I got the message too late and I was already here." I told her my story and she bought it hook, line, and sinker.

I just wanted to get her talking so it wouldn't look too obvious that I was fucking her man. By the time we reached Michael, I had Roses laughing like we were old friends. I could tell Michael was nervous seeing both of the women he was fucking together in his face.

But this was going to show if he knew how to 1) Either go with the flow or 2) Be a typical man and fuck himself by getting caught up. To my surprise, he was quick on his feet and knew the philosophy of the survival of the fittest.

"Hey baby! What are you doing here?" He said to Roses as he kissed her lips.

17

"Well, I just wanted to see my husband and I decided to surprise you." Roses answered.

"I see you and Jade have met, I hope she didn't tell you I was being mean to the kids." Mike said playfully tapping me on my back. Before the conversation could continue the offensive coordinator called him on the field to call a play.

Roses and I watched him run to the middle of the field. I turned to Roses and said to her, "We should get together for lunch and shopping?"

Roses smiled and said, "Yeah girl we should, you might be alright to go out with and shoot the breeze with!"

"Well let me give you my cell number so you can call me whenever." I went in my back pant pocket, pulled out my business card, and handed it to her.

"Well, let me go! I have errands to run. It was nice to meet you Roses." I said as I turned to walk away.

When I got to the car, I made up in my mind; I was going to have them both as my lovers. I had no intentions of breaking them up. I just wanted them for my pleasure and I prayed that no one's feelings got in the way.

July 7, 1986-Entry 3

I have been sleeping with Michael for eight months and we began to venture out into the public as a couple. We would go to the outskirts of town for dinner and other activities, but my desire was to be with Roses.

It had been about three months since she and I had met. It was now time to make my next move. I had Mike believing I was satisfied with our arrangement. Truthfully, I was content with our arrangement, but I wanted his wife.

Since, I hired the PI, I found out everything about Roses; from her daily routine to who her OB doctor was. I knew she was out of school for the summer break and did not have to go back until the end of the summer. It was time for us to have another random encounter.

Mike told me last week that he could spend a few more hours with me, because Roses was going to get her yearly pap exam. Little did they both know, Roses and I had the same OBGYN.

Dr. Washington and I knew each other on a more intimate level that extended beyond the doctor/patient confidentiality clause. It was time to pay Dr. Washington an office visit. It had been almost a year since we last saw each other, but she will always hold a special place in my heart.

I called her office the week before Roses' doctor appointment.

"Dr. Washington's office how may I help you?" The receptionist stated into the receiver.

"Yes, Dr. Washington, please." I requested.

"I'm sorry Dr. Washington is unavailable, may I take a message?" She asked.

By this time I had no patience for the bullshit. She didn't know who she was pissing off. If she wanted her job she was going to transfer me to her boss a.s.a.p.

"Look, whoever you are, I know Vivian is in her office!!! You tell her that Jade wants to speak with her. If you do not put me through; honey you will be on the soup line faster than what you think...so please don't test me, because I don't make idle threats!" Before, I could catch my breath, I heard Vivian saying "hello" on the other end.

"Well, hello stranger. Long time, no talk too." I answered back.

"Look, Jade, we haven't seen or talked to each other in about a year, and now, all of, sudden you call to my office! What is it that you want!!!?" Said to me, but I could tell from her voice that she was more surprised than upset.

"Well, Vivian, I was thinking about you and I

wanted to hear your voice. Besides, it's getting close to the time for my annual visit with you. But enough about me, really, how have you been?"

Although, she and I hadn't spoken in quite some time, Vivian had never been far from my thoughts. Sometimes, I wondered if we truly could have worked out for the better.

"You could have set an appointment with the receptionist. It wasn't necessary for you to speak with me." Vivian said.

"Well truth be told, I would like to see you, for old time sake over drinks. So, why don't you let me send a limo for you and we can go to your favorite steak house. I already made reservations for us." I knew if I came with honey she would bite like sweet nectar.

"Ok, Jade. Have the car at my house by 8:30." With that said she hung up the phone.

With the confirmation of my anticipated date, I finished the last of the paperwork on my desk. I ordered the limo and took the rest of the day off. I needed to look good for tonight. I needed a fresh manicure and pedicure.

After my appointment at the day spa and a bite to eat, I went home to get ready for the evening. I decided to wear my Ralph Lauren black pinstripe pant suit, with a red see through camisole. I wanted Vivian to see my hard nipples through my shirt.

My heart shaped diamond Tiffany necklace, earrings were my accessories, and on my feet I wore black opened toed high heel Coach Shoes. I had a busy night ahead and I needed to be on my "A" game.

The limo was at my house by eight and we were pulling up to 1563 Trailblazer Drive by 8:20. Vivian walked from her house with a sultry strut and a flawlessly made face. The sight of her made me want to taste her. When she got in the limo, we greeted each other with the usual pleasantries.

"Well good evening lady. You look absolutely stunning!" I told her, trying hard not to lean over and take her in the backseat. "Thank you. You look good yourself." She said.

As we rode to the restaurant, we talked, but I could not help myself... I wanted her.

I grabbed Vivian by her face and began to kiss her lips. She was surprised by my actions but didn't resist me. I slowly kissed her neck and fondled her breasts. I moved my hand down her inner thigh and separated her legs. I needed to get my hands inside her secret garden.

Her moans of pleasure in my ear made me want her

even more at that moment. I licked my finger and placed it on her clit. I began to manipulate her clit in circular motions; then I placed my thumb inside her pussy. I felt her juices coming down my hand.

I whispered in her ear, " Baby, don't come too soon. I want to feel your sweet juice in my mouth."

As I was talking in her ear, I was sliding her black thong down her legs. I placed her right nipple in my mouth and slowly sucked it. She threw her head back in ecstasy.

Vivian laid flat on the seat and placed her legs over my shoulders. I licked and sucked her clit. I licked and sucked her until she was about to pass out.

"Vivian do you want Bobby?" I asked her.

Vivian looked at me and said, "Please baby give me Bobby...ohh baby I want him." She told me.

I already had Bobby, my double headed dildo on. I pulled down my pants and placed Bobby in me first. My pussy was throbbing so hard that I had to ride him first.

Wanting us to both come, I placed the other end inside of her. We rode until we both got off. I wasn't done yet. I wanted my pussy eaten. I got on top of Vivian's tongue to let her taste me. That one thing I missed about her; she always ate my pussy until I almost had a seizure. By the time we finally got to the restaurant we both worked up an appetite.

After dinner, we made love over and over again for the rest of the night. It was four in the morning by the time the limo picked her up from my house. But I had accomplished my mission for the night. I got in Vivian's good graces and I walked away with a doctor's appointment on the same day as Roses.

July 14, 1986-Entry 4

Today was the day I was going to see Roses at the doctor's office. I was so excited; I had been dreaming of her while I was in the arms of her husband. Although, I wanted Roses, I was not about to stop sleeping with her husband. I had been fantasizing about this "so called" chance meeting for the last week, and now it was time for action. My appointment was at 2:15 and hers was at 2:30.

I arrived at Vivian's office at two to get a jumpstart on my paperwork and to my surprise Roses was early as well. She saw me first. She came up to me and started talking.

"Hey Jade! Are you here to see Dr. Washington as well?" She said as she walked over to sit next to me.

"Well hello there. I haven't seen you at practice in a while." I responded back to her.

24

"Well that was a one time pop in. I'm not that involved with his football team." She stated.

"Mrs. Jenks, Dr. Washington is ready to see you." The nurse technician called from behind the doors leading to the examination rooms.

"Maybe we can still have lunch soon Roses." I said to her as she rose from her chair. She smiled and said, "Yeah we need to get together. I still have your number. I'll give you a call real soon."

After she went through the doors, it was time for me to go to work. I got up and pretended as if I was going to the ladies room. I went through the doors that led to the exam rooms, and went straight to the lab where the blood work was tested. I looked for Roses' vial of blood. I took her vial and placed it in my purse; replacing it with a vial from my coat pocket.

On my way out, I bumped into one of the lab techs. She looked at me and asked what I was doing in the lab. I said, "I'm sorry I got confused and made a wrong turn coming from the bathroom. But I think I hear my name being called for my appointment." I said continuing on my way.

Since all follow-up appointments were done a week after the exam, Roses' and I would be back again; at the *same place at the same time next week. I just needed to wait for the shit to hit the fan.*

After my appointment with Vivian I went to see Michael at our hideaway spot. I had to break him off some pussy before I met Vivian at her office for a quick rendezvous.

When I got to her office, she was seeing her last patient of the day, so I waited patiently in my car until she called me on my mobile to let me know she was done for the day.

After an hour of waiting, the call came. I stepped out of my car wearing nothing but a long spring coat with black pumps. I wanted to get the show on the road and I didn't need clothing getting in the way.

I rang the doorbell to the office building and was buzzed in. I walked directly to her office and opened the door. Vivian was sitting at her desk writing notes. I immediately dropped my coat revealing my naked body. I could see she wanted to play the hard role and not look too eager to get it on with me.

I walked to her desk and flung everything to the floor. She looked up at me with an angry face.

"What the hell are you doing?! These are my patients' information you're throwing." She said. I didn't

respond. I picked her up, placed her on the desk, and put my wet pussy in her face.

She was reluctant at first, but I made it very apparent that I didn't have time for the games. I was there to get my rocks off by any means necessary...even if I had to take it from her.

"Vivian, do what you do best and you better do the shit now! All the other bullshit can wait until later." I told her in a stern voice.

She took her thumb and forefinger; opened my pussy lips, and placed her hot tongue on my clit. She licked and sucked on me until I erupted in her mouth with my passion.

After I was satisfied, I sat in her office chair and told her to sit on my lap. We began to kiss and I fingered her until she was about to cum. I yanked her by her jet black, silky, shoulder length hair, and pulled her down on Bobby. She moaned from the intense pleasure. As she rode me, Vivian played in my pussy. She and I both moved in a unison beat of passion, sex and ecstasy...together we came.

After our escapade, we laid on her desk to catch our breath. I looked into her eyes and realized just how beautiful Vivian was. The first time we tried to develop a relationship I couldn't appreciate what she was able to

offer me, because she was too needy. I didn't want her to
have deep feelings for me, because we were casually dating
and she's married with children.

"Look Vivian, we need to discuss some things
before we go any further. We need to clarify things between
us." I said to her.

We sat up and looked at each other. I grabbed her
hand and began explaining to her how it was going to be
between us. "Look, "V" we tried this once before. I know I
stop dealing with you without giving you an explanation. I
need to tell you why." I said. I could see the fear in her
eyes; I wanted to approach the conversation with as much
tact as I could.

"I'm listening, because I do miss what we shared."
She said.

"The truth is Vivian, the first time around; I felt that
you were too needy and insecure in our relationship. The
excessive calling and showing up to my job unannounced,
all that shit was not cool! In fact, the shit was scary!" I told
her.

She looked at me with her puppy dog eyes and
said, "I know. Before, I was so attached to you. You gave
me something that my husband can never give me." She
stated.

I had to put some of my cards on the table if I wanted my plan to work. "Listen Vivian, I like spending time with you, and the sexual chemistry between us is undeniable, but I need you to understand our relationship is strictly casual…meaning you have a husband, children, and a career. I have a life, a career, and I see other people." There was a pregnant silence in the room before I spoke again.

"The bottom line is, if we are going to see each other, you need to go with the flow. You need to know that we won't see each other everyday, and I'm not going to call you every minute of every hour. But the time we spend together will be just us…doing what we do; and no it's not all about us sleeping together either. I just need you to feel what I'm saying." I told her.

She kissed me, told me she understood, and that she would comply with my wishes.

July 21, 1986-Entry 5

I waited in the empty exam room for Roses to finish her appointment with Vivian. I knew it would be longer than usual. When she walked out of the office, I wanted to be the first person she saw. It was now 3:15 and Roses had been in Vivian's office for 45 minutes. By this time, I was ready for her to come out.

Just when I was getting frustrated, I saw the office door open and Roses walked out. She was visibly upset and had been crying. As she was walking past where I was, I opened the door and literally bumped into her on my way out the door.

"Oh, I'm sorry! I didn't see you coming! Roses is that you?" I said playing it off. She looked up at me with a tear stained face; fell into my arms, and started crying uncontrollably. I quickly pulled her back into the room and sat her in the chair.

"What's wrong luv? Why are you upset?" I asked already knowing the answer. She looked so fragile, as if she was going to have a nervous breakdown. I wanted to console her, but I didn't want to come on to strong. I needed to be the shoulder she could lean on in her time of need.

"Oh my, God! Michael has been fucking around on me! I've been married to this man for five years and I never thought about stepping out on him! This is what the fuck he does to me! That bastard!" Roses ranted in one deep breathe.

"How do you figure he is sleeping with someone else besides you?" I quizzed. She wiped her tears from eyes and pulled herself together.

"I know because, Dr. Washington just told me that I have an STD. She said

"Well maybe your lab work was mixed up with someone else's. If I were you, I would get a new test done just to make sure the results are correct." I told her.

"I've already ordered the blood-work to be redone, but I know that nigga is cheating on me. I've known for almost a year, but I never said anything about it. I was brought up to stay with your man, especially if he takes

care of home." Roses stated.

I looked at her, took her in my arms, and hugged her. I knew she needed one.

"Look, I know this may be an awkward moment for you, but you need to get this off your mind. Why don't you let me treat you to lunch? We could go to Chilli's and get some drinks." I asked hoping she would go with the flow and say yes.

"Why sure you can treat me to lunch, and since you are inviting me, I hope you're paying?" She said laughing. I looked at her and began to laugh too. It was good to see a smile on her face. Although, I was plotting to get her between my sheets; I still wanted her to be happy whenever she was with me.

It was now 10:00 p.m. and we had been together the majority of the day. We went to lunch and dinner. We even went to the mall and picked up a few pair of suits and shoes. Now we were at my house having drinks to recap the day's events. I went over to my stereo and put on Anita Baker's album on the turntable. The album began to play and the first song that came across the speakers was Sweet Love.

She and I sat on the couch enjoying the music. There was a strong vibe between us. I don't remember asking her to dance but what I remember next, was us slow dancing in my living room. Our bodies connected in a sensual and seductive way.

To my surprise, she made the first move. Roses began to hold me closer to her body, and moved her hand down the center of my back. She lightly grabbed my left breast. I was taken back by her actions, but I didn't reject her advances. Once I knew she was comfortable, I leaned down and kissed her softly. She returned my kisses by slipping her sweet tongue down my throat.

We began taking each other's clothes off. At that moment, I was in state of euphoria. I looked at her and said, "Are you ready for me to turn you out, because after tonight you will want to see me again." The smirk on my face said it all.

Roses responded by putting both of my nipples in her mouth and sucking.

"Damn, baby, you getting me ready to take you!" I shouted. Without any other further delay, I started to find my way to her virgin pussy lips. When my face was between her legs; I looked at her pussy and wrapped her legs around my back.

I went to work on her like I was going mad. All I heard were her moans in my ears. I sucked and licked her until she convulsed, releasing her pussy juice in my mouth. I wasn't quite done with her yet. I led her to my bedroom. Once we were in my room I went to the bathroom and got the KY.

"I need for you to let your mind be free and for you to relax your body." I told her.

"Jade, you can do whatever you want with me. I'm yours for tonight." She told me.

I placed the KY on my finger and placed it inside of her ass. I strapped Bobby on and turned her on her stomach. I got on top of her and played with her pussy. I grabbed Bobby with my left hand and played in her pussy with my right hand.

I eased the tip of Bobby in her ass. She tensed up from the initial pain.

"Baby, trust me all I want to do is make you feel good. Just let go!" I assured her.

I started pumping her ass with Bobby and as she moaned I was also moaning, while the other end of Bobby was going in and out of me. Roses, was enjoying herself so much that she began throwing it back to me.

I made love to her all night long. When the morning came I sent her home to her husband. Before she left we made love again. Right then and there, I knew, she was going to be in my bed from then on.

The Present.........Mikleah

"What the fuck!!!!! I can't believe my mother was such a whore!" Mikleah screamed as she jumped out of the bed. All of her life she held her mother in such a high esteem that she could do no wrong. But now to read her mother's words in her own hand writing was mind boggling to the comprehension.

Ross was awoken by Mikleah's screams. "What's wrong Baby! Why are you screaming?" She asked while she reached for her clothes.

Mikleah looked at Ross and responded, "Nothing baby, I will be ok. I just needed to scream, but I'm alright now. Where do you think you are going?" She asked deflecting the attention away from herself.

"Tomorrow I have an 8 a.m. class and my day will be hectic because Wednesday is one of my busiest days at school, so I'm about to leave." Ross answered.

"Damn you just going to fuck me and leave, that shit is cold!" Mikleah said laughing.

"Now, baby you know I would stay if I could. You know how I feel about us, but I can't have my head between your legs and keep my head in the books too." Ross said

also laughing.

After she made sure Ross was in her car Mikleah went back in the house and took a shower. As the water ran down her body, her tears were drowned by the streaming water from the shower head. Her thoughts went to her happy childhood and how her mother was such a good mother to her. Never in a million years would she have thought the worse about the one person who loved her unconditionally and always had her back.

After the long shower, Mikleah emerged feeling emotionally drained. Since her mother's passing, she took the semester off from school so she could regroup. Financially she was secured and never had to worry about money. When Jade died she left her a trust fund worth $5 million dollars and a 3500 square foot house that had been paid off by the insurance money.

She couldn't believe how similar she and her mother were, all the way down to them both enjoying pussy. She had no idea that her mother was such a sexually free person. The similarities between them were undeniable.

It was like dajvu. Jade, was reincarnated in Mikleah once she was born. Although, she was thoroughly disgusted by her mother's diary she could not stop reading it. It was if Jade was speaking to her from beyond the grave. Mikleah sat at the dining room table, and turned to the next chapter of the diary. She was turning the pages of her mother's secret life.

Caught Up
Chapter 2

December 24, 1987-Entry 6
One Year Later

One year of jugging multiple lovers has begun to take its toll. Although, I got what I wanted both Roses and Michael... I was the one finding myself wanting to be with Roses on a more permanent basis; especially now the holidays are here.

I wanted to take her to see my family and enjoy her company. I knew the rules to the game; the other woman always got the day before or the day after the holiday.

I arranged to have my gift delivered to her house, since I knew she was out of school for the winter holiday. I sent her a two-carat right hand ring from ZALES jewelry store, with a sentimental letter attached.

To The Woman of My Dreams,
I know that you will be thinking of me this holiday. I wish we could be together. Since we can't, I just wanted to give you something that shows you how much I care. I ONLY WANT YOU TO WEAR THIS RING FOR ME AND NO ONE ELSE!!
Have yourself a Merry Little Christmas and we will be together soon.
                                        Jade

Although, I was not going to be with either Michael or Roses, I was going to enjoy my time with my family. But for the year 1988, I had plans, big plans. So I will take this time for myself and recuperate. I will need all of my strength for the trials that will be ahead in the New Year.

The Set Up
Chapter 3

January 14, 1988-Entry 7
One Month before it went down.................

Today, I bought three first class airline tickets to sunny Miami, Florida. I plan to invite my two favorite people with me for an explosive Valentine's Day getaway. The tickets were for February 12th, 13th and 14th. I wanted to ensure my guests would be accompanying me, so, I FED EX the tickets with a note explaining why their presence would be necessary.

I sent Michael the February 13th ticket to his locker at work with a note saying:

My Dearest Michael,
I know you want us to spend more time together. I would like to make your wish come true. I have arranged for us to vacation in the Sunshine State for the Valentines Day weekend. Enclosed is a first class roundtrip ticket with paid expenses on me. All you have to do is bring yourself.
Now, if you decide to decline my offer be prepared for your dirty little secrets to be aired in public, and I don't just mean you sleeping with me......
I will see you there in The Sunshine State.
P.S: How do you think your boss will react once he finds out you fucked his wife and 16 year old

daughter.....Damn you couldn't find an adult... don't worry how I know, but there is plenty more where that came from....

Jade

I sent Roses the February 14th ticket to her classroom with a note saying:

My Sweetheart Roses,
I have a surprise for you!!!!!! An all expense paid trip to Miami exactly one month from today. I know you are probably wondering what you are going to tell your husband, but I wouldn't worry too much about him. You are a smart lady and I'm sure you will come up with something. Besides, if I don't see you there, I will be forced to tell some things about you, that I know you want kept private. For Example: What would your husband think if he knew you aborted his son? Or if your mother knew you were fucking her husband- your step-father for years and you just stop last year?
I'm looking forward to seeing you next month.
P.S: How could you stoop so low to screw your family... that shit is disgusting?

Jade

I knew my threats to both Roses and Michael would not fall on death ears and I was getting ready for the backlash...

January 14, 1988-Entry 7 cont.............
5:15 p.m.

Here comes Mike storming through my office door demanding an explanation.

"How in the hell do you know about me and my boss' wife and daughter, and who the fuck do you think you are going to tell this too?!!" Mike said to me with tears of anger in his eyes.

I reared back in my chair and cocked my head to the right with a look of dominance on my face. I knew t he was scared shitless. He wanted to take his demons to his grave. Mike knew he would lose everything even his freedom if it got out that he had sex with a minor.

"Look, baby your secrets will be safe with me as long as you oblige my request. I'm quite sure you no longer want to be involved with me and that's fine. I just want to say goodbye to you on good terms with no hard feelings." The "BS" kept coming out of my mouth.

Mike looked at me with the look of pure venom in his eyes. I knew in my heart that he would truly be devastated by losing his wife.

"I'm telling you Jade; if you tell my wife about the sins I've committed in the past; I will come for you with a vengeance. I know what I've done was wrong and foul, but *the shit is in the past where it should be! Now, I'm regretting even getting involved with your psycho ass!!!" He spat back at me.*

"Oh, so because I pulled your cards.... now you regret you got involved with me! Nigga please! I did not force you to do anything you did not want to do. You weren't concerned about hurting your wife or anyone else...that's "BS", because if you were for real about trying to keep your dirt in the past, you could have ended this a long time ago. So what you need to do is leave my office before I call security and have your ass arrested for trespassing." I told him with all of the strength that I could muster.

As he walked out of my office, I walked up behind him, grabbed his arm, and turned him towards me.

"Get your fucking hands off me...you trifling bitch!" Mike said to me.

"If you are thinking about telling your wife or quitting your job in order not to come to Miami, I will be sending your brother an anonymous letter stating he should get a paternity test for the son who belongs to his younger brother." My statement took the breath from his body, and with that said I watched him walk out of my office.

8:00 p.m.

The entire day passed and there was no word from Roses. I was surprised, but not shocked. I kind of figured she was going to be stubborn, but I knew she would be on the flight to Miami.

Michael

"I can't believe this shit!! This gutter slut is trying to blackmail me! Unbelievable!" Mike yelled as he slammed the door to his Cadillac.

"I knew the shit was too good to be true, something had to be wrong with the bitch!" He was so livid that he could hardly think straight.

As he rode to the bar, he began to wonder how Jade knew about his deep dark secrets. His brother's wife was his girlfriend before she married Keith. When they finally decided to call it quits, Sade was seeing both of them and she ended up pregnant.

They both lied to Keith, telling him that they stopped fucking around six months before she got pregnant. Deep down, he always had the gut feeling that Jordan was his son. He was too much of a coward to ask for a paternity test.

44

As far as Charlotte, his boss' wife, the affair was brief. Now, Kim his boss' daughter was a different story. He met her at a company function and they flirted. But she would not let it be. She would come to the office to flirt with him. It was like the more he resisted her advances the more she would pursue him.

Finally, one day when her parents were out of town for business she invited him to the house. He knew he was violating, but curiosity got the best of him. From the first time he stuck his dick in her tight pussy; he knew he could not stop fucking her. Still, to this day they still had relations from time to time.

He felt trapped in the situation with no where to run. He was not about to expose himself or broadcast his secrets. So he would make the trip to Miami. He prayed that they could both go their separate ways without them coming to blows. But he knew that was wishful thinking. The best thing he could do was let her think she was in control until he was able to come up with an alternate plan of action.

Straight With No Chaser
Chapter 4

February 12, 1988-Entry 8
Miami

On my flight to Miami, I had an anxious feeling in the pit of my stomach. Although, my nerves were rattled, I was determined to complete what I had put into motion. Around 2 p.m., I arrived at the Miami International Airport and was driven by limo to the Westin Resort Hotel. Upon my arrival, I paid for my penthouse suite and the two luxury hotel suites that were equipped with all of the amenities of an exotic resort.

After carefully examining both Roses and Michael's rooms, I went to the 20th floor to my piece of paradise. The room was absolutely beautiful!!!! I could see all of Miami from the terrace. The room was tastefully decorated with a Bohemian theme. I decided to relax in the Jacuzzi and release my tension.

It was after 10 at night when I got in bed. My mind was filled with visions of Michael and Roses. They were so vivid in my mind; it was like they were in the room with me. I could not wait for the next day. With a smirk on my face and my hand on my clit, I went to sleep with the sweetest dreams in my mind.

Michael

Today was the day, February 13th. Michael had been dreading this day for a month, but now it was time to face his fate with Jade. He told Roses he had a job related conference in Charlotte, NC.

His flight was to depart at 12 in the afternoon and he was to arrive in Miami at two pm. He was walking to the boarding gate when he heard the announcement for all passengers for flight 102 to Miami. After going through security Mike gave the ticket person his first-class boarding pass for the flight.

He had to admit Jade had class. He had never taken a flight in first- class before.

"Sir, would you like a drink?" The stewardess asked. "Yeah, let me get a White Russian." Mike told her. He definitely needed a drink, because he had no idea what was in store for him once he landed in Miami.

After he got his drink, Mike got his carry-on bag from the over head compartment, and retrieved the letter Jade sent him. The letter came to his job a week before the trip. He wanted to the read the letter again to see if there were clues to what the real was as to why Jade invited him to Miami.

Michael,

When you arrive at the Miami International Airport there will be a limo waiting to take you the hotel. There will be no need to check in because your room has been paid for. Your room key will be in the limo in a manila folder.
I have made dinner reservations for us dine at an Italian restaurant. After some grub, we're going to the booty bar for entertainment. The rest of the night will be ours. See you in Miami.

It seemed as if she had the trip planned to a "T", but he knew it was more to it than what she was saying. Although, Michael was in suspense about his adventure, he was also excited. He prayed to God the night before that he would not regret the decision to make the trip. As far as he was concerned, Jade had his life in her hands. His life as he knew it, could soon be crumbling down around him.

"Ladies and gentlemen we will be landing in Miami in approximately 10 minutes. Please fasten your seat belts, enjoy your stay in the beautiful city of Miami, and thank you for flying Delta Airlines." The pilot announced over the intercom. It was time to face the music.

February 13, 1988-Entry 9

Michael's flight arrived on time. I had to put on my game face. I knew, I had all of the aces in my favor, and *this trip was going to accomplish everything I wanted. The day ahead was planned.. I sent room service and a bottle of Moet champagne to Michael's room. I wanted to show some hospitality and make him as comfortable as possible.*

I had just gotten out of the tub and decided to call Mike's room. I went over to the bed, picked up the phone, and dialed room 1010. "Mike, how are you doing luv"? I asked as soon as he answered the phone on the second ring.

"I was lying on the bed and enjoying my beautiful room that you have provided for my pleasure." He said.

"I just got out of the tub and I'm all clean. I was wondering if you would grace me with your presence in my room." My voice was low and seductive. I could tell he was down for some action, but he was hesitant, because he didn't know what to expect. He was silent for a long moment.

"Look, Mike I know you are wondering why you are here, but I promise my intentions are good. So, why not come to my room in 20 minutes so we can have a discussion before our dinner date. I'll see you in room 2013 in 20 minutes." I said as I hung up.

After I hung up, I got up from the bed and put on my clear stripper heels and a blonde wig. I wanted to spice things up with him and roll play. I pulled out my collapsible poll and mounted it directly in front of the king sized bed. My time was running thin so I had to hurry. I went back into the bathroom and sprayed on my Beautiful perfume and checked my make up. I was ready for him.

Just as I was leaving the bathroom I heard a knock at the door. Just before answering the door, I went to the closed closet door and turned the camcorders on that were hidden strategically around the room. I greeted Michael at the door with my nakedness.

"Welcome to paradise!" I said as I stepped to the side to let him in.

"What's up with the wig?" He asked as he kissed me on the lips.

"I'm sorry Jade is not here. I'm Passion and I'll be taking care of you while you are here in paradise. Now let me get you a drink. Please have a seat in the chair right over there." I directed him as I sashayed my ass over to the bar. As I fixed his rum and coke, I grabbed the remote for the stereo that was mounted in the wall and turned on a mixture of slow songs.

I wasted no time getting into my role. After giving him his drink, I began to slow wind for him moving my body seductively to the music as it played. Michael's eyes were watching me with desire. I went to the poll and jumped on it and began to swing around it.

"Damnnn...baby! You are working the shit out of that poll! Let me get out my money, because I definitely got to tip you!" Michael yelled out. He began to throw 20's and 50's in the air at me.

I was in such a zone that I began to make my ass clap in his face. Mike started to smack my ass. Having his hands on my ass was making me hot. I climbed on top of him for a lap dance and began to undress him. My kisses were hot and wet on his body. We started to kiss passionately. I jumped off him and kicked the chair from underneath him; causing his body to fall to the floor.

"You know I like it rough, but I don't do carpet burns on my ass." He said with a little chuckle. I looked at him and turned around and placed my ass directly in his face. He grabbed my ass, rubbed it, and kissed it. I could feel his fingers finding their way inside of me. I could do nothing but ride them. I moved back and forth. It felt so good that I let out a moan. I pulled his fingers out of my pussy and sucked my juices from his fingers. His dick was rock hard; I knew he was ready, and I was ready for the real thing.

I led him to the bed and he laid back placing his

head on the pillows. I crawled to the edge of the bed and placed my mouth on the head of his dick. I sucked him until he was ready to explode. Not wanting him to cum yet I placed my pussy in his mouth to let him feast in my bush. I threw my head back in pleasure.

He was eating me like he was a mad man. His tongue was all over my clit. I couldn't help myself I began to tremble as I felt my juices coming to a head. I busted off in his mouth, but he wouldn't let me get down so I could ride him. Michael grabbed my hips and began to pull my pussy to his mouth. Not wanting to disturb the mood, I just went with the flow and let him feast.

After, I came two more times we fucked all over the room for about two hours. After our episode we both laid in the bed and listened to the music coming from the speakers. Finally, after about 10 minutes of silence, Michael turned, looked me in my eyes, and said, "Jade, if I wasn't married, I think I would have been with you. You have your hooks in me in a way that I can't explain and I don't just don't mean the sex. You stimulate me on many levels." There was such sincerity in his eyes that I almost felt bad for sleeping with his wife.

"Michael, I have been dealing with you for the last two and a half years, and I never expected this relationship

to continue this long. But, now I think its time to go our separate ways so you can be faithful to your wife. With me out of the way you can concentrate on being a better husband." I said as I got up to take a shower.

"Why don't you come take a shower with me, I want to enjoy this time together." With that said we both got up and took a long steamy shower filled with more sex. Not wanting to waste the rest of day in the room, we went to our dinner reservations and to the strip club for entertainment. I paid two girls to give Michael lap dances and to fuck him.

Of course, I was going to watch all of the action. At about three in the morning, the limo came to pick us up and we headed back to the hotel. We all ended up in the penthouse. We had more drinks and an orgy. The shit was awesome. We all enjoyed ourselves. When the morning came, the two girls were gone and I kicked Michael out my room, because, I had to get ready for Roses.

As I was getting in the shower, I knew my life was about to change. This was the first time Mike and I had slept together without using protection. Right then, I knew, I was pregnant.

■■

February 14, 1988-Entry 10

Roses' plane was scheduled to land at 1:30 this afternoon. I was up early. I ordered breakfast and sent beacon, eggs, grits, and pancakes to Michael's room. I needed to keep him occupied until later that night. I called to tell him that I had a female escort waiting for him downstairs in the limo. She would show him the rest of the city and give him some love. I made sure to tell him to be at my penthouse around one in the morning.

After making sure Michael was gone for the rest of the day, I prepared myself to meet Roses at the airport. I dressed in a chic but classy all purpose black Ralph Lauren dress. I put on my Tiffany diamond necklace, bracelet, and diamond studs for my accessories. On my feet were open toed Nine West Heels. I was able to get a fresh manicure and pedicure that morning from the spa on the first floor of the hotel. The limo was at the hotel to pick me up at 12:45.

I was nervous to see her, because it had been awhile since we had last seen each other. Before I left home, I purchased another two-carat ring for Roses. But this time, the ring was a commitment ring. I wanted to be committed to her and only her. I was at the airport at one to pick her up.

When I saw Roses walking down the terminal I

could not stop thinking how stunning she looked. She was wearing skin-tight jeans, a silk blouse with three buttons opened exposing the top of her breasts and six-inch heels. I couldn't help but notice that she was wearing my ring on her hand.

"Hi, Roses how was your flight"? I asked her. I could tell she was perturbed about being in Miami.

"My trip was fine, but I know I'm here for business and not pleasure." She said as she stopped in her tracks and faced me in the middle of the airport.

"I can't believe you would go through such extremes to dig up my deepest secrets and threaten to expose them to the people who are the most important in my life! Lord knows I have not been perfect. I have my sins to bear! How can you claim to love me and want to be with me and still you hurt me in this way?" She was so upset that she had tears in her eyes.

I looked in her eyes, grabbed her face, pulled her lips to mine, and kissed her. "Look, Roses I'm sorry I threatened you with the information that I know about you. I would never hurt you. Do you know how much I love and want to be with you? I know you think that I'm out to hurt you, but I'm not. I just needed to ensure we could be together." I said.

"So threatening me is going to help us be together? All you've done is push me further away from you and not towards you. You didn't need to do any of this; I was already yours for the taking." Roses said. I was speechless and hurt but I couldn't display my hurt.

I reached inside my purse and produced the Tiffany box. "Look, Roses I know you are upset with me. I have missed you and I want to make it up to you. I brought you this." I gave her the box.

She looked at the box and smiled. Her eyes widened once she opened it and saw the ring.

"What is this for"? She asked as she put the ring on her finger.

"I want us to be together on a permanent basis." I told her as I grabbed her hand and began walking to the awaiting limo.

At the restaurant Roses and I made small talk, but I needed a drink to calm my nerves. "Yes, I would like an apple martini with salmon and vegetables as my meal." I told the waitress.

"And for you ma'am, what you are eating?" The waitress asked as she turned to Roses.

"I'll have the same." She answered. As the waitress walked away with our menus she and I talked. I explained

to her that I was not going to use the information that I had against her. We talked about our relationship and about our feelings for each other. After our meal we went back to her hotel suite for passionate love making.

February 14, 1988-Entry 11
One Hour before the Showdown
12:00a.m.

Before I left Roses' room I left a note inviting her to my penthouse suite at 12:30. I was ready for whatever. I took a quick shower and put on my red negligee from Victoria Secret and sat on my bed.

At about 12:20 there was a knock on the door. As I walked to open the door for Roses, I made sure that everything was in place. "Roses come in. I've been waiting for you." I said to her as I left the door cracked for Michael. With no hesitation we picked up right where we left off. She began kissing me and leading me to the bed. She opened a bottle of champagne that she brought with her and poured it over my body.

Roses licked the liquid from my body and we started to bump our bodies together. Her body felt absolutely wonderful pressed against mine. Roses turned me over on my stomach. As she was kissing my back, she made her way down to the center of my ass. She pulled me to my knees

57

and started to lick my ass furiously.

I was in a trance. I started fingering myself and as Roses was tossing my salad she fingered her pussy too. We were both on cloud nine and had not realized Michael entered the room.

"Roses, what in the hell are you doing?" There was a sound of undeniable anger in his voice as he grabbed her from between my legs.

"I asked you what the fuck are you doing here fucking her?" Michael repeated as he grabbed Roses by her arms. Before she could answer the question I jumped off the bed and stood next to them. I looked at Michael and flipped the shit back on him.

"You see what she is doing! The million dollar question is what are you doing here?" Roses looked at me and looked at her husband with a confused look on her face.

She slapped his hand away from her body and smacked him across the face. "I can't believe this shit! You mean to tell me that you have been fucking the same woman that I have been with!!! That you have been eating the same pussy that I have! How can this be?" Roses was upset by the revelation and the hurt was in her eyes.

I saw the distress in her eyes and I immediately

wanted to comfort her from all the pain she was feeling. I unconsciously grabbed Roses and kissed her. This infuriated Mike and he pushed me away from her. I was upset that he put his hands on me and I flipped.

I looked at the both of them and said, "I don't know why the both of you are standing here as if you two are running things here! Neither one of you are running shit around these parts! On the real, I've been fucking the both of you for years! Yes, I make your wife scream my name every time I lay it down! You can't satisfy her in the ways that I do! So, let's stop the games, because you both know I hold the key to everything you hold dear!" They both looked at me with disgust but I didn't care.

"Come here Roses." I said to her. She looked at me and wouldn't move.

"I said bring your ass over here to me!" This time she came to me. I put her right nipple in my mouth and licked and sucked it until it was erect. I pushed her down on the bed and began to eat her out. Although, she was agitated she couldn't help but throw her head back in ecstasy. There was no need to wonder where this was going, because Mike was already jacking off.

He grabbed my ass and stuck his dick in me. He felt so good. As tensions started to fade, we emerged into our threesome. We all pleased each other. After Mike fucked me, he went to Roses, and started to fuck her slow. Not wanting to miss any of the action I put my pussy on Roses' tongue and let her devour me. The three of us had a passionate night of sex. But, in the morning, it would be a new day and there was going to be questions that needed to be answered. In my eyes, the trip to Miami was a success. I had accomplished what I set out to do……get my girl.

The Present…..Mikleah

"Oh, my God!" Mikleah said in a voice that was full of shock. She could not believe what she was reading. There were so many questions going through her head. How could her mother be so manipulative and vindictive? What she was reading was not the woman she knew. The pages of her mother's diary were not reflective of the woman who was her protector, friend, and caretaker. The pages of her mother's diary showed a selfish woman who would stop at nothing to get what she wanted.

As she sat at the dining room table trying to compose herself, the doorbell rang. When Mikleah looked through the peephole she saw Rosslyn.

"Hey baby. What are you doing here?" She asked as she opened the door.

"*Well, I thought I would stop by and spend time with my girlfriend. I have been worried about you.*" *Ross said as she walked over to the bar and poured them both drinks.*

"*Look, Ross you know I've been grieving over my mom's death and I've been reading her diary. I just don't know how to handle the type of lifestyle my mom was living.*" *Mikleah said.*

Ross looked at the first woman who she had ever been intimate with and thought how much she was in love with her. They started off as friends from college. Time progressed; she and Mikleah became secret lovers. They both were afraid their families would disown them; they kept their relationship a secret for over a year.

"*Look, baby I think you need a break from this diary. Why don't we go out on the town tonight? It will be my treat.*" *Ross asked.*

"*I know you only want to see me happy. I don't think I want to go out tonight. But, I do have an idea, let's order Chinese food and watch a movie on demand.*" *Mikleah said as she went to the phone to order the food.*

"*Well, if that's what you want to do, then I'm down. You can order me a large combination of Sweet and Sour Chicken with an Egg Roll.*" *Ross responded.*

They both got comfortable on the couch with their food and watched Tyler Perry's Daddy Little Girls. They spent the rest of the night on the couch. It was a nice mental escape for Mikleah. Although, she was not reading the pages of her mother's diary; her thoughts went to the possibility of locating the man she never knew...her father. But to find out where she came from she had to finish reading the diary.

Drama and Relationships
Chapter 5

The Morning After

"How long have you been sleeping with Jade, Michael"? Roses asked her husband.

"You have some fucking nerve to ask me how long I've been fucking Jade, because you have been fucking her just as long as I have! So don't come with the self-righteous bullshit!" Michael shouted back.

Roses and Michael were both shocked to find out that they were both having an affair with the same person. Michael was even more shocked. He could not believe his wife of five years was not only cheating on him, but she was cheating on him with another woman. The same woman he had been fucking for two years.

Although, he had to admit the threesome they had was off the hook; he had no idea how he and Roses were going to get past their infidelities.

"Look, Roses all of my cards are on the table. You know what I've done; just like I know about your deeds. You are my wife and I made a vow to God and to you. I married you until death do us part. There is no excuse for what I've done but we can work through this together." His

eyes showed the window to his soul and at that moment....he was vulnerable.

Roses looked at her husband. He had been having a two year relationship with another woman, but she still loved him and wanted to be with him. She just couldn't forgive and forget so quickly.

"No, Michael I can't see how we can move on from this. You have betrayed me and my trust. Right now, I want you to pack your shit and get the fuck out!! By the time I come back, I want you gone!" Roses got up from the couch; grabbed her purse, keys, and walked out the door.

Once Roses was gone Michael sat on the couch and thought about how he could have been so blind to the fact that Roses and Jade were sleeping together. He had to admit Jade was slick. He had been under her spell for far too long, and, because he was weak; he was about to lose his wife over some pussy. It was going to take time for the wounds to heal, but he was committed to getting his wife back.

Roses drove with tears streaming from her eyes. She was crying so hard that she could hardly see the road. She pulled to the side of the road.

"Oh, my God what have I done to my life!?" She said as she wiped the tears from her eyes.

"I have been sleeping with the woman who has been sleeping with my husband." She said out loud.

She was so confused about her feelings. It was true that she had love for Jade. Hell, she was still wearing her ring. Once Roses was composed she got back on the road and continued the drive to Jade's house. She needed to ask her why.

Jade was home having a White Russian thinking about the trip to Miami. She knew she had taken a risk by revealing that she was sleeping with both Roses and Michael, but it was the only way to separate them. She knew that once the secret was out in the open; Roses would kick Michael out the house, and she could slowly get back into her good graces.

While pondering her next move, the doorbell rang. She looked at the clock and it read 11:30. "Who could be coming here at this time of night?" Jade said out loud as she got up from her king-sized bed to open the door. She opened the door, saw Roses, and was at a lost for words. She stood there with the door open not saying a word.

"Are you going to invite me in or not?" Roses said as she brushed past Jade walking into the house.

The two women sized each other up before either one of them said a word. There was a sense of anxiety between them. They were still attracted to each other, but the circumstances from the night before made it hard for them to connect.

"Why are you here? All of your issues should be taken up with the person who you have a commitment with." Jade said as she sat down in the chair.

"How could you hurt me? I thought we were building a relationship fostered on trust. How can I be with you when you stooped so low and fucked my husband?"Roses needed her questions answered.

Jade looked at Roses and began to laugh. She was tickled, because she still didn't get it. "Roses, yes it is true, I've been fucking Michael way before I started sleeping with you. But, what you don't understand is, once I saw you for the first time; I knew I had to have you. So yes, I did what I had to do. If exposing you and Mike's secrets or showing you that your husband was having an affair with me was what I needed to do; then you're damn right, I did it!" Jade walked over to Roses and got in her face. She wanted her to see how serious she was about what she wanted.

"How could I have been so blind to trust you? You have done nothing but turn my life upside down! You say that you love me but you don't give a fuck about me! All

*you care about is yourself and getting your pussy eaten!"
Roses said.*

Jade pushed Roses to the floor and got on top of her pinning her down. Roses tried to get from underneath her grip, but Jade overpowered her.

"Stop moving I am not going to hurt you!" Jade said. After a few minutes Roses finally stopped moving and looked in her eyes.

"You can't tell me that you don't love me, because you do! I know you are hurt, but that will soon pass. If you didn't want me or want to be with me, you wouldn't be here pleading your case." Jade was so turned on by Roses' panic that she began to kiss her lips.

Roses resisted at first, but Jade was right she did love her. They began to kiss. As much as Roses was fuming with disgust for Jade she could not deny the desire in her heart. The love they made that night transcended all of the brokenness of her shattered heart. In the arms of Jade was where she felt safe and secure. At that moment she felt that this was where she needed to be, and not with Michael.

"Jade, I do love you!" Roses screamed as Jade went down on her. They made love beyond Roses' wildest dreams. The love making was more intimate. They tasted each other's juice and expressed their deepest desires.

In Roses' mind she knew she couldn't be with Michael and she needed to be with Jade. Jade catered to her every sexual need. Jade took the time to learn her body and what turned her on. It had been a long time since Michael showed her that he was truly in tuned with her sexually.

After their sexual episode the two women held each other until the morning. "Jade, I do want to be with you, but I don't know if I can trust you." Roses said to Jade as she kissed her. Jade walked to the kitchen to cook breakfast. The words that came from Roses' mouth pierced her soul.

Although, she got want she wanted, which was Roses, she did not want them to have a trust issue. It was true; she had done some foul shit, but it was all done in the hopes of her being with Roses.

"Roses, I will be honest with you. From the first time I saw your face, I knew I had to have you. I will not apologize for anything that I have done. I saw a woman I wanted, and I had to get you by any means necessary." Jade said.

Roses, was in shock from the events of the last few days, but she was ready to commit to Jade. "Jade, I wear your ring because I want to be with you, but I can't be with you if you are going to continue to run game on me." Roses said to Jade.

"Roses, I promise you this, I will be straight up with you and I will not ever hurt you. I love you girl! So let's just take it one day at a time." The two women kissed to affirm their commitment. They ate breakfast together and spent the rest of the day in bed.

March 14, 1988-Entry 12

Roses and I have been practically living together for the last month. Lately I have been feeling sick and nauseated. I have been hiding my morning sickness from Roses by vomiting in zip lock bags and throwing them out on my way to work. Although, I own my own business I still feel the need to be at work everyday to make sure that shit was getting done.

It was time for me to see Vivian. I needed to see how far along I was. Since, I was carrying Michael's baby I decided to keep it, and raise the baby with Roses. I called Vivian's office and set an appointment for the following *week.*

Lately, I have been noticing that my baby has been moody and more tired than usual. In my heart, I knew we were in the same boat....pregnant. I hadn't mentioned to Roses that I detected the raised levels of HCG in her blood. I will not tell Roses right away that I'm pregnant. I know, that us, having children from the same man will be very stressful. Hopefully, we will be able to weather the adversity and raise our children together as siblings.

March 21, 1988-Entry 13

My doctor's appointment with Vivian was a touchy situation. I had a late appointment. When I walked into the office I had an overwhelming feeling of guilt, because once again, I have faulted on my verbal commitments. Now it was time for me to feel her wrath. I walked into the examining room praying that all was well with the baby.

"Well, we meet again."   Vivian said as she motioned for me to sit down on the exam table.

"How have you been V?" I responded back with a nervous tone in my voice.

"So tell me what brings you to my office?" Vivian asked.

"I need an ultrasound. I think I'm with child." I told

her.

Vivian was taken back by what I told her. She sat down in the chair across from me with the look of devastation and shock on her face.

"So you mean to tell me, that a woman who claims to have her shit in tact got knocked up! Not to mention, that once again, I have been the biggest fool to ever believe that you were serious about giving us a fighting chance to develop a relationship. But, I have no one to blame but myself and all of the mistakes have been my own. So let's not prolong this and see how far along you are." Vivian said as she put on her latex gloves.

I felt so bad for my broken promises, but I could not change what was done. "Vivian, please believe that I never meant for any hurt to come to you. I truly had all intentions of being with you; just other things got in the way." I said.

"You know what! Please save the bull for your baby's father, because at this point I don't give a damn. Lay back, so we can get this over with, and we can get on with our lives." Vivian's voice was stern and I never heard her speak that way before.

"It looks like you are about five, almost six weeks pregnant." The screen showed the first signs of another human being growing inside of me. My emotions were *mixed. I was happy and scared all in one.*

"I advise that you watch your diet and begin taking prenatal vitamins. Also, I am passing your information over to Dr. Hamilton. From now on, he will be your practicing OB." Vivian said as she handed me the prescription for the prenatal vitamins.

Although, I was wrong for all the lies I told; I was unprepared for this kind of backlash. Before I could protest the sudden change in doctors Vivian walked out the room and into her office. I knew I had burned a bridge and all that was left was a woman's scorn. I got dressed and placed my first ultrasound picture in my purse.

The walk to the car was the longest walk ever. Feelings of sadness kept entering my spirit. Once again, I had left another lover feeling like shit. Now that I was pregnant- I was praying that none of my imperfections would rub off on my unborn child. The ride home was the longest ride ever. I wanted a drink, but under the circumstances that was out of the question.

Roses

Roses hadn't seen nor spoken to Michael in the past few weeks. She had been happier with Jade in last weeks than she had been with Michael within the last year and an half. Jade didn't know that she knew she was pregnant. Roses would pretend to be sleep in the morning as Jade got dressed for work and she could hear her vomiting in the bathroom.

What made the situation more complex was that Roses was also pregnant. Roses knew she was pregnant when she missed her period last month. Her period came like clockwork every month and when it didn't come, she knew what the deal was. It was confirmed when she took the EPT.

In her mind, she knew the father of their children could only be Michael. Roses kept asking herself; did Jade set the shit up so she could get pregnant with Mike's baby or did the shit happen accidentally? She couldn't trust Jade, but she couldn't force herself to leave.

Roses needed to find out what she had gotten herself into with Jade. For the time being, she decided to continue playing like it was all good until she could figure out her next move. Before, she could go any further; she needed to go to Dr. Washington and ensure that the baby was fine. This time she wasn't terminating the pregnancy.

Roses, was stunned when she left Dr. Washington's office. Dr. Washington told her that she was entering the eighth week of pregnancy. This revelation meant that she had gotten pregnant before she went to Miami.

She still had not told Mike or said anything to Jade. Today was the day she was going to let the cat out the bag. Roses had enough of the games that she and Jade were playing. It was time to tell Mike that he was going to be a father.

She called Mike to let him know she was stopping by the house so they could talk.

"Hello, Michael. How have you been?" Roses asked.

"I have been fine and how about you?" Michael answered.   "Well, we need to talk. I have some things I need to get off my chest. I will be stopping by the house around seven. I'll see you in a few hours." With that said Roses hung up the phone.

Michael

Michael was not expecting to hear from Roses. It had been over a month since he had seen or talked to her. The word on the street was that she was shacking up with Jade; playing wifey to his mistress. Nevertheless, he was happy to hear from her. He still had hopes of reconciling their marriage. One thing about Roses, she was stubborn, and it would take time for her wounds to heal, but he knew she still loved him.

Since he was staying at the house without Roses he started seeing Kim again. Now, she was at the legal age of consent, and sleeping with her wasn't considered statutory rape. Kim was a killa in the bed, she gave some mean head, and she was always down for anal. They were careful, because they could not afford for her father or anyone from the job to know.

But, now it was a possibility that Roses wanted to talk about getting back together. Mike was excited that she was coming by. He needed to get the house together. He went through the house tidying up. He went to the kitchen and cooked them, T-bone steaks, baked potatoes, baked beans, garlic bread, and salad. While dinner was finishing he showered and shaved.

He dressed in black Polo slacks, a cream polo shirt, and black and cream Stacy Adams. He dabbed a touch of Calvin Kline Obsession cologne on. He went to the mirror and looked at his reflection. Michael thought to myself, damn I'm sharp! He went to turn on some music, poured a shot of Hennessy, and waited for Roses to arrive.

Ding Dong!! The door bell rang. He looked one last time to make sure that every thing was ready before he opened door. Ding Dong!! "Well let's make this happen."

He said to his reflection in the mirror.

"Good Evening Roses, how are you doing tonight?" Michael said as he opened the door to let her in.

"I've been well and how about you Michael?" She said to him as she entered the house that she once shared with him.

As Michael looked Roses over he realized that there was a certain glow about her. There was something different; he just couldn't put his hand on it.

"Things are going alright over here. I just don't have my wife at home." He said.

"Well we have some things we need to discuss tonight. Trust me there will be plenty of time for us to talk about the state of our marriage." Roses said to her husband.

Roses and Michael sat at their dinning room table to eat. The night was going well as they had casual conversation. The suspense was getting the best of Michael. He needed to know what exactly was on his wife's mind.

"Roses, I know that we are not going to spend the rest of the night having small talk. There is a reason why you wanted us to get together, so what's up?" He asked Roses as he leaned back on the couch.

Roses grabbed her husband's hand and looked in

his hazel eyes. Her demeanor became intense and her eyes got misty. "Michael, I know we have been through a lot within the last few months. We both have done our dirt, but it's not just about us anymore." She said.

Michael was hearing what she was saying, but he wasn't sure if he understood the context of her words. "What do you mean it's not about us?" He asked.

"I'm pregnant and we will be parents in October!" Roses shouted.

Michael's first thought was that October was seven months away which meant Roses was already two almost three months into her pregnancy. The shock of her words made him jump from his seat. The emotion that was running through his body was beyond any known words.

"So you wait two months to tell me that I'm going to be a father! Why wasn't I your first call!?" Mike asked his wife.

Roses looked at Michael and could tell that he was genuinely hurt by not knowing sooner.

"Look, Mike I wanted to make sure that I would be able to carry the baby. The first trimester is when a woman is most likely to miscarry. I just wanted to make sure that the baby was ok before I told you the news." Roses said.

"That is such bullshit and you know it! So do you

plan to come home so we can be a family? I will not allow
you to let another woman or man raise my child! Look
Roses, I'm so sorry that I hurt you. I know I was wrong for
sleeping with Jade, but I want us to move past this. There is
an undeniable love that is still between us. The two of us
have been through the fire." Mike was pleading with his
wife for her forgiveness.

    Roses saw the authenticity in his eyes and saw
straight to his soul. She knew the desire in her heart for
Jade was strong, but was it strong enough for her to turn
and walk away from her husband?

    "Michael, I understand what you are saying. It's
true that we have been through a lot together, but how can
we get pass this?" Tears were now streaming down Roses'
checks as she spoke. She was filled with an emotion from
deep within her soul. She loved Jade but she was still in
love with her husband.

    At that moment, Mike decided he was not about to
let his wife return to the arms of his mistress. He picked his
wife up from where she sat and carried her to the bed they
once shared. He kissed her lips and kissed her tears from
her eyes. He crawled in the bed next to her and moved her
close to his chest.

    All he wanted to do was hold her in his arms, and

make her feel safe and secure. He knew he had to start first with an emotional attachment.

"Look baby, all I want to do is hold you in my arms tonight. I know we can make it work, but tonight, I just want you to close your eyes, and rest all of your cares on me." His hazel eyes were warm and caring. Roses could feel his love. They laid in the bed not saying a word until they finally fell asleep.

May 11, 1988-Entry 14

It had been two weeks and Roses had not come home. I knew she was with Mike playing house. I was overwhelmed with anger. My heart was mutilated and I was bitter. I felt like a fool! I had put all of my eggs in one basket and now the cat was out of the bag. The one who I wanted betrayed me and our relationship.

I was pissed and all I wanted to do was strike back at both Roses and Mike. I know I have my faults. I have done some foul shit, but my intentions were pure. I came to the conclusion that it was time for me to leave and go somewhere where I could get a fresh start with my baby. But, before my departure I needed to extract my revenge on those who hurt me….starting with Roses and Michael.

It was now time to reveal all that I knew about both of them, but first I wanted her shit out my house. I went to my stereo and put in Eric B. & Rakim, Big Daddy Kane and Doug E. Fresh. I needed to hear something to get me pumped and ready for war.

The songs of Ain't No Half Steppin, I Ain't No Joke, and Keep Rising To The Top played loud threw my speakers. I started going through the house throwing Roses' shit in a box. All the while I was thinking to myself that Mike will be shocked to know that he will be having two babies instead of one. Not to mention all of his darkest secrets will be revealed.

By the time I was finished packing all of Roses' things it was almost 11pm, and yes, I had no intentions of prolonging getting her things to her.

Although, I was almost three months pregnant I was not yet showing, and I hadn't gained much weight. I could still get into my clothes. It was time to pay the happy couple a visit. Before my unexpected visit I needed to get ready. I went to my bedroom and took out my sexy Victoria's Secret red Strappy-back baby-doll, my silver open toed platform shoes, and laid them on the bed.

I wanted to freshen up so I jumped in the shower and washed my hair. After my shower I sat at my vanity and applied my makeup flawlessly. After my makeup was applied I pulled my hair back in a pony tail and put a clip-on ponytail in my hair.

I put my J'adore lotion on my body and slowly got dressed. My adrenaline was pumping and my pussy was secreting my juices. I was turned on by what I was about to do and started tasting myself. After a few thrusts into my *pussy with my fingers I was now ready to head to my destination.*

I arrived at the Jenks' household by midnight. I parked my black E320 Mercedes a half a block down from their house. I got the car and strutted the rest of the way to their front door. With my light jacket open and box in my hand; I held my head up high, rang the door bell, and waited for the door to open........................

Back to the Present...........Mikleah

Mikleah had been reading her mother's diary for over a month. She had learned more than she wanted to know about her mother's life, but now to find out that she had either a brother or sister, that shit was mind boggling.

No one in her family, including her mother, ever uttered a word. The truth was one of those dark family secrets that would be taken to the grave, but this secret was going to come to the light, because she wanted answers.

She grabbed her car keys and drove to her grandmother's house. Kleah was going to her nana and confronting her about what she knew. Her mind was set on one thing- getting answers.

She arrived at her nana's house and started on her quest for the truth. "Hey nana how are you doing today"?

She asked her grandmother as she gave her a kiss on the cheek.

"Hey, baby how have you been? I haven't seen you in a few days where have you been"? She asked as she fixed her tea and sat down at the kitchen table.

"Well you know nana, I have school almost everyday. So I haven't been having the time to come and see you, but I'm here now. I came by here to talk with you about my mom." She told her as she sat down next to her at the kitchen table.

"Well what do you want to know about Jade, sweetie? What's on your mind Mikleah? What is it that you what to know"? The look in her grandmother's eyes said it all. She could tell she knew it was time for her to come clean about her mother's other life.

"Nana you know when my mother died that not only did she leave me her business, her house, and a hefty life insurance policy; but she also left me her diary. Her diary has shown me insight into another life that my mom had, and it's revealing to me so many aspects of her life that was once hidden from me. Now, I have to know the truth." She said as her voice pleaded with her for understanding.

Jamison had reared two daughters and had raised them to best of her ability. After the death of her husband *she was left to be mother and father to both Jade and Jaylyn. Both of her girls were straight "A" students, popular, and involved with every extra curriculum school activity there was. But when Jade turned 15, she started to notice a change in her.*

A mother knows when her child is no longer a virgin, but with Jade it was different. It was like she was addicted, and she was ready to explore every aspect of her sexuality. As a mother she tried to talk to her, but her voice went in one ear and out the other. Because of Jade's sexually free spirit there were numerous heart breaks and drama.

Jamison looked at her grand-daughter and was dreading the impending conversation that was about to occur. "Baby, tell me exactly where you are coming from." She asked as she sipped from her tea.

Mikleah was afraid of what she was about to hear from her nana, but she needed to know the whole truth behind the words that were written in her mother's diary.

"Nana, is it true that I have a sister or brother that I don't know about?" Mikleah asked her grandmother already knowing the answer to her own question.

"Kleah, let me start off this conversation by saying that Jade loved you more than life itself and when you were

84

born she changed her life around. Baby, your mother was a woman that was a sexual deviant. Ever since she began having sex she was addicted. I tried my best to keep her from sleeping around, but my best efforts were to no avail. But, finally, she was getting her life together. Jade slowed down for awhile, and was able to open her marketing firm." Jamison was weary about telling her too much before she had the chance to read it first in Jade's diary.

"Nana, I know all about how momma was a good mother. You know just as well as I know that behind that pseudo of hers that she was living a double life. Yes, she was good at hiding it from me, hell I had to learn of this other life by reading her diary! But, all I want to know is do I have a sibling-yes or no?" This time she was in no mood for a long drawn out story about her mother, because right now her mother was looking more and more like a high class whore.

"Baby, look your mother was who she was. We all make our mistakes in life, but we learn from them, and try not to repeat them. All that I can say is that there was a time when Jade was interfering in a relationship that she had no business in. After time feelings got involved, and as always, Jade wanted what she couldn't have. Because she couldn't let go and move on, she decided to open Pandora's

Box. Kleah, because your mom was obsessed with getting what she wanted, she caused turmoil in her life and the lives of others who she sought revenge on. Her manipulation was the reason why you were never told that you have a brother or sister in the world." Jamison was saddened by what she revealed to her grand-daughter, but she was also relieved. She knew that keeping the truth from Mikleah would do more harm than good. Kleah was a strong young woman and she deserved to know the truth.

Mikleah took all that she heard in stride. She was glad her nana kept it on the up and up with her. She would have been devastated if her nana had looked her in the face, and told a bold face lie.

"My nana, I know this was hard for you, but you don't know how much the truth means to me. I love you nana." Now that her fears were confirmed it was time to finish her mother's diary so she could find clues to who her sibling was. Mikleah was determined more than ever to find her missing half sister or brother and try to form a relationship with them. She knew in order to fulfill that goal she needed to read the diary to the last page. There was no time to waste.

After, her talk with her nana, she was determined to find anything tangible that could lead her to the identity of the sibling that she just found out about. Mikleah started her endeavor by first going to her mother's bedroom.

It had been almost three months since she stepped foot into her mother's room and she was feeling overwhelmed with emotions. Mikleah could feel her mother's presence surrounding her. After a few minutes of reminiscing about the many nights that she spent with her mother talking with her on her bed she was ready to embark on her investigation.

The first place she started to look was in her dresser drawers. After carefully looking through the dresser, night stands, and the armoire she came up empty. Feeling a little defeated she sat on the bed and looked at the closet.

She went to the closet door and tried to open it. To her surprise it was locked. After a closer examination of the door she realized that a key was needed to unlock the door. Her eyes scanned the room. Mikleah was thinking where she would have put the key.

She went back over to her dresser and looked through her things that were on top. Mikleah was so anxious to find the key that she knocked over a box that had a pair of diamond studs in them.

When she picked the box up she felt something taped to the bottom of the box. "Hmmm... could this be what I'm looking for?" Mikleah thought as she turned the box upside down to examine the hidden contents.

"I'll be damn. I would have never thought to look under this box for the key. This just goes to show how slick my mother was when it came to hiding her dirt." She thought as she placed the key in the closet door to open it.

Once inside the massive walk in closet she did not notice anything out of the ordinary. As she walked to the back of the closet she noticed that there were several plastic storage boxes stacked neatly off to the side of the wall. There were two small boxes and three medium sized boxes. She decided to pull the boxes one by one out of the closet into the living room so she could see what was hiding in the boxes.

The opening of the first two boxes yielded what seemed like hundreds of VHS video tapes. When she opened the rest of the boxes her eyes widen when she saw a variety of sex toys from dildos, rabbits, strap-ons, anal toys and so forth. She picked the rabbit up and wondered how often her mother used it.

"Damn mom!!! I guess it's true what they say that the freaks do really come out at night!!" She said out loud. Right before she was about to place the contents back she came across an envelope with some negatives and a safe

deposit box key.

Right then she knew that she had found something that was going to aide her in her quest. Looking at all of those toys had her juices flowing. "I think I'm going to pay my girl Ross a visit and take some of these toys with me so we can a have an all night long session." She said as she got up to place the call to Ross.

May 11, 1988-Entry15……….Cont

When the front the door opened the shock on Michael's face was priceless. His eyes showed lust, shock, and fear all in one. "So are you going to let me in or let me stand outside?" I asked him breaking the momentary silence.

"What the fuck are you doing at my house Jade? What do you want?" He asked with a tone of sarcasm. Before I could respond Roses came to the door to see who her husband was entertaining at the front door.

"Jade, what are you doing here at this time of night?" She asked as she stood next to Mike at the front door.

I looked at both of them with the look of pure venom and said to them, " If the two of you do not want a scene out here in your front yard, I suggest you let me in, because

I have no problem showing my ass for all to see." With that said they both stepped aside and let me enter the house. Once inside, I wasted no time getting to what I had come to do.

I walked through the foyer and into the living room area where I dropped the box holding Roses' contents. "What are you doing here Jade?" Roses asked again as she walked up to me.

"I'm here to return your belongings since they will be no longer needed at my place of residence. Or have you forgotten that you were just in my bed not too long ago?" I told her with a smirk on my face.

Michael entered the room and stood behind Roses. "Look Jade, Roses, and I, have both came to the conclusion that we both fucked up, and we're trying to work out our differences for the sake of our child. The time you had with my wife has come to an end and its time for us all to move on." He said.

I looked at Roses and I could see in her eyes that she still had feelings for me and that she wanted to be with me. With Michael standing there, I walked up to his wife and looked her in the eyes, and asked her the most imperative question that was on all of our minds.

"Roses, do you want to be with me? Think about the

question before you answer, because from the look in your eyes, I can see the truth."

Before she had a chance to answer the question, I immediately placed my tongue in her mouth and began to finger her pussy. It seemed like an eternity since I last kissed her lips and felt her creamy insides. Suddenly, I felt hands grab my arms and I was pinned to the couch.

"Jade, you have some fucking nerve to come into my house, and in front of me try and seduce my wife. What kind of sick and twisted bitch are you!!!" Michael screamed as he held me down.

I looked at him and said, "I'm that bitch who can fuck you and your beloved wife anytime I chose! You are just mad that you found out that you were not the only one I was sharing this pussy with, and to add insult to injury I turned your wife out!!!! Nigga, I suggest you take your hands off of me, because I have a mind to call the police and file domestic abuse charges on my jealous lover!" My words resounded loud and did not fall on deaf ears, because Michael released me and stood in silence.

My intentions were to belittle him and remind him that I held the power over his wife. Once Mike released his grip I dropped my coat to reveal what I had on. Both Roses' and Michael's eyes got wide and lustful. No one uttered a word, because the both of them where mesmerized by my masturbating.

As I licked my fingers I began to plunge my fingers one by one in and out of my sugar walls. As I pleasured myself I could see Michael rubbing his manhood. I moaned with such passion and seduction.

"Roses, don't you miss this pussy? Don't you miss touching, licking, and fucking this pussy?" My words were getting the best of her because she went over to Mike and got down on her knees, unbuttoned his pants, and placed his big black dick in her mouth.

Her tongue stroked his shaft up and down. She rolled her tongue around the head, and deep throated him. While she was sucking him off, I crawled over to Roses and parted her legs and started my expedition in pleasing her wet crevices.

The three of us engaged in another threesome that solidified that we would always be intertwined. Roses turned and kissed me slowly. We relished the taste of each other's lips. We explored each other's bodies and expressed our sentiments.

"Bend the fuck over Jade so I can fuck you!" Michael said as he pulled me by the hair and bent me over. Although, Mike was being extremely rough, his roughness *turned me on even more.*

With my face down and ass up Mike smacked my ass and rubbed his hand on my pussy. I enjoyed his touch, in fact I longed for a male's touch. He pushed his manhood in me, and I moaned from the pleasure I felt with each lunge of his curved dick.

Michael grabbed my head and whispered in my ear, "You think you are slick coming here with the intentions of fucking my wife and breaking up my home. This will be the last time you ever touch my pussy in your pitiful life!"

He fucked me until he could not stand to look at me any longer. Once he was done he squirted his bodily fluid on my breasts. He turned and walked away leaving me and Roses alone. She looked at me and the fright was written all over her face. Before we spoke any words, I got up and retrieved my jacket and headed toward the door.

I could hear her following behind me. I opened the door to make my exit when Roses called out to me, "Why are you out to hurt me?" She asked.

With one hand on the door I turned and looked at her. "Why I'm I trying to hurt you? You have the audacity to ask me this! All that I've done, I've done to be with you, and to make a life with you! But, you turn around and slap me in the face! You know, I have no one to blame but myself, but it's all good. You and Mike can have each other, because two trifling whores deserve each other."

With that said I opened the door and headed to my car never looking back.

It was over for now, but when it was time to strike back it was going to come with the fire and brimstone of a woman scorned who was out for vengeance. As I drove my car away, I realized, I was leaving the one who I wanted to be with. I would let them play the happy family and when they least expected it their world would come crashing down.

How Life Changes But Vengeance Remains the Same
Chapter 7

November 1988-Entry 16

November 21, 1988 was the day that my life changed for the better. I delivered a six pound baby girl whom I named Mikleah Rose Jackson at Emory University Hospital in Atlanta. She was perfect and my love for her was a love that I had never experienced before.

After our stay at the hospital I took my baby home. She and I started our new lives in a new city where no one knew me or about my sorted past. This was one of the best decisions I made in my life. I had left my company to my sister to run in my absence and I took a job as VP of an up and coming PR firm. As long as I was going to live in Atlanta I was going to make the best of it.

I kept my PI on my payroll to keep tabs on Roses, Michael, and the new addition to their family. The PI sent me a picture of the baby and the resemblance to my child was striking. Now that the children were in the world I knew that the time was not right for me to extract my revenge.

I was going to have to bide my time and wait for the

perfect moment to attack. Until such time I had all intentions of living my life and taking care of my daughter. Christmas was right around the corner and then the New Year will be rolling in. It is now time to get things started in the right way, but soon and very soon vengeance will be mine.

The Revelation
Chapter 8

The Last Entry…..Entry 17
2007

My Dearest Mikleah,

As you know I have been keeping this diary for the better part of 20 years. When I found out that my days with you were numbered, I made a conscience decision to let you into my world… a world that I tried so hard to shield from you. So, I left my diary for you to read once I was gone. I know the entries that you have read have given you a new perspective about me.

But, I want you to know that you are my daughter and I love you with everything that is within me. All I have done was to protect you, and to give you the best life that I could have possibly given you. I know that if you are reading this letter that you have read my diary in its entirety. Now is the time for you to get the answers to all of your questions.

This is what I want you to do. First, I need you to go to my lawyer, Angela Martinez's office, and she will provide you with an envelope. That envelope will contain keys to a safe deposit box. Do not open the box until all of your questions have been answered. Angela will be expecting you, so you don't need an appointment.

Mikleah, in all that I have done, I never wanted to hurt you or cause you any pain. ALL of the mistakes have been my own. I know that I raised you to be a strong and independent woman who could handle anything that came her way. Now will be the time for you to dig down deep, and show what you are made of.

Remember that you are Mikleah Rose Jackson. Baby girl, know that I love you, and I never wanted anything, but the best for you. Once the smoke clears, and all has been revealed please forgive me and don't hate me.

My Love For You Will Be With You Always,
Mom

Back to the Present….Mikleah

The tears flowed down like when the heavens above pour down on an afternoon with a rainstorm. The more Mikleah tried to wipe the tears the more they streamed from her eyes. She was heartbroken.

She had finally come to the end of the diary, and her emotions were in a tailspin. The woman who cared for her all of her life was gone, and she was all alone to fend for herself; and to discover that she had a sibling that she never knew about; was overwhelming for anyone, especially a 20 year old.

It was all so surreal and stressful. Mikleah needed a release from her reality. What she needed was a fat blunt to smoke on. She went to her cell phone and paged down until she reached the number she was looking for. She dialed Todd's number.

"What's up boy!?" She said.

"Shit, nothing right now just chillin." Todd said as he fired up his weed filled swisher sweet.

"Since you aren't doing anything why don't you come over and let's smoke one. She asked.

"Alright, give my 20 minutes and I'll be to the house." He said as he hung up the phone.

Mikleah had known Todd for years and they always had a close relationship. Although, they never tried to take their friendship to an intimate level, they always remained cool. She pulled herself together and waited for her company to arrive.

It had been a few weeks since Todd had heard from

Mikleah. Mikleah was his closest female friend and they got closer once her mother passed. He could tell from the sound in her voice that she was upset and needed to smoke to relax her mind.

The distance to Kleah's house was a 10 minute drive. Todd rode with the window down of his black Range Rover as he bumped his music. He puffed and thought about the first time he laid eyes on Mikleah. When he saw her he was instantly drawn to her beauty. Ever since then they had been the best of friends. They were just not the kind of friends who had benefits.

He had finally arrived at his destination. Todd gathered his shoe box which held the weed and blunts needed for their get together. Todd rang the doorbell and waited for Mikleah to answer. After what seemed an eternity the door finally opened.

"What's going on girl!" Todd said as he embraced Kleah in his arms. The two of them walked to the living room and sat on the couch.

"Todd I'm so glad that you came over. I've been going through a lot and I just didn't want to be alone right now." Mikleah said as she rolled the weed in the blunt.

"Well your boy is here to save the day. So tell me what's on your mind." He said as the blunt was passed to

him. Mikleah let the weed take it's affect on her mind and body. She felt all of the stress and tension leaving her body. It was just what she needed... a tranquil atmosphere where she could get her thoughts together.

"Boo, you know I have been going through it since my mother died. I have been maintaining, and living my life, but the more I read her diary the more I realized I was getting deeper into a world I had no idea about. Now that I have finished the diary, my mother left me some instructions. It's just that I'm so afraid of what I'm going to find out." She said as she inhaled the shotgun that was being given to her.

Todd was also feeling the weed. He digested what his friend told him and wondered to himself, what other secrets Kleah's mom had. "Kleah it's up to you whether or not you are ready to find out the truth. I mean do you really want to know? Or do you think you want to know?" He said.

The question that was posed to her left her pondering. She knew in her heart of hearts that she needed to know the truth. Mikleah knew she would always want to know the truth.

Todd and Mikleah chilled and smoked the rest of the night. They listened to music, poured some drinks, and

101

smoked weed. The vibe between them was one of sexual attraction coupled with a mutual respect for the friendship that had evolved between them. The two of them smoked the rest of the night and eventually fell asleep on the couch together.

It was a wet Wednesday and Mikleah was just getting out of bed. She had decided to play hooky from school. She didn't want to deal with the weather. This was a prime opportunity for her to start her journey to find the truth. As she bathed in the shower, thoughts of what she was getting into entered her mind. Not only was Mikleah nervous, but she was also afraid of the truth.

It had been a few weeks since she last seen Ross, and she missed her. She had become so engrossed in reading her mother's diary that she had not found the time to see her. She decided to stop by Ross' apartment before heading to Angela Martinez's office.

She picked up her cell phone and called Todd. "What's up Todd!?" She said as Todd answered the phone.

"Nothing, right now. I just got in from making a run. What's going on with you?" He asked.

"I just wanted you to come and pick me up so you can go with me to an appointment." Kleah said as she put on her Baby Phat jeans.

"Alright luv. I'll be there to pick you in an hour. So be ready to go when I get there." Todd told her as he said bye and hung up the phone.

After dressing Mikleah went to the kitchen, fixed some food, and sat at the table to eat. As she was eating the door bell rang. She looked at her watch, and thought damn, Todd got here quick. Mikleah got up to open the door and to her surprise it was not Todd; but Ross standing there with the look of a mad woman.

"Damn girl! You must have been reading my mind, because I was going to stop by your house before my appointment." She told Ross as she stepped aside to let her in the house.

"Cut the bullshit Kleah! I haven't heard or seen you in like three weeks and now you say that you were coming to see me today! If you don't want us to be together at least be a woman about the situation and tell me to my face that you don't want to be with me! I have given a 100 percent to this relationship, and all I have gotten in return is nothing." Ross hollered at Mikleah.

Ross was in love with Mikleah and wanted to be with her. They had been together for a little over a year. Mikleah was her first relationship with a woman and she knew from the first time that they were together that she could never go back to dick...she was officially turned out by the pussy.

Mikleah looked at Ross and she loved it when she was mad. The sex was always off the chain especially after an argument. But today, at this moment, she didn't have the time or the patience to deal with her.

She grabbed Ross by the arm and pushed her down on the sofa. "Look Ross I'm sorry that you have not heard from me in a few weeks, but I have been going through some things that I needed to deal with by myself! If you can not understand that, then maybe you are not who I thought you were! You know you're the only one that I'm sleeping with! If I was fucking someone else I would have told you straight up. So don't come to my house screaming that shit about me not wanting to be with you!" Mikleah said as she took another bite of her sandwich.

Ross looked at her lover and took in every word she had heard. She knew she was wrong to come at her like that. Rosslyn knew that Kleah was going through a lot since her mother had died. She did not want to add anymore stress to her already stressful life.

Ross walked over to Mikleah and bent over to kiss her. Just the touch of Kleah's lips made her want her even more. "Look baby, I'm sorry for coming at you so hard. It's just that I've missed you and I want to spend more time with you. When I don't hear from you I automatically assume the worse." Ross said as she grabbed her nipple and began to manipulate it until it got hard.

Mikleah allowed Ross to continue rubbing her nipple. She was in need of a sexual release. In the back of her mind she knew she had to hurry before Todd came to the house. She grabbed Ross by the hand and led her to the sofa.

She pulled down her clothes and put her freshly shaved pussy in her mouth. Her tongue felt so good on her clit. Mikleah began to get into it and began to move her hips to the rhythm of her tongue.

Ross ate Mikleah with a fever pitch of perfection. She released all of her bottled up frustration into her mouth. Kleah exploded like hot lava from a volcanic eruption. She grabbed her breast and let out a loud scream as her love came down.

Ross licked all of the juices that flowed from the inner place of Kleah's soul. Ross was more than happy to relax her woman. When she was done enjoying her orgasm; she got up, went to the kitchen for a paper towel, and wiped herself. The doorbell rang as she was cleaning herself up. This time she hoped it was Todd coming to pick her up.

Todd and Mikleah arrived at the lawyer's office at four and they checked in with the secretary. The secretary walked to Ms. Martinez's office and advised her that she had a client waiting in the lobby. Ten minutes later Angela was walking toward them.

"I'm sorry to keep you waiting Ms. Jackson. It is so good to finally have the opportunity to meet you." She said as she extended out her hand.

"Thank you for seeing me without an appointment. This is my friend Todd." Mikleah said as she introduced Todd to her as well.

The three of them walked to her office. Once inside, they sat and the meeting commenced. "Ms. Jackson let me start by first saying that I am truly sorry for the loss of your mother. Jade was one of my long-term clients. I also considered her a good friend and she is truly missed. Your mother left specific instructions for me to carry out once you were finished reading her diary." Angela stated as she leaned back in her chair.

Mikleah was surprised that she knew about the diary and wondered if her mother had fucked her too. Today, she was not there to learn anymore about her mother's sexual encounters, but to get answers to her questions.

"Ms. Martinez, as you know, my mother directed me to you. Her diary informed me that you are the link between me and some of my mother's loose ends. I am ready to find out the truth." Kleah said.

"Ms. Jackson, the only thing that you need to do is wait for your mail. Everything else has been taken care of. Once your questions have been answered, you can come back to my office and pick up this envelope." She stated as she stood from behind the desk.

"So you mean to tell me that this has been a waste of time. I won't be getting the package today! You could have told me this over the phone!" Mikleah said as she stood up to leave the room.

"Mikleah, before you go, please do not be upset. I'm only carrying out what your mother wanted. She knew the key in the envelope would be needed once you learned the truth. I'll walk you to the elevator." Angela said as she opened her office door.

Angela made sure they were on the elevator before making her way back to her office. She closed the door and walked over to the mini bar. She poured herself a glass of vodka with pineapple juice.

She sat at her desk, unlocked the drawer, and pulled out five large manila envelopes. Angela knew that the shit was about to get thick. She knew Jade's daughter was going to be in for the shock of her life, but she just didn't know it yet.

Angela raised her drink skyward and said, "Jade you are one bad and ruthless bitch." She said as she poured a few drops of her drink on the floor.

Michael…..3 months After Jade's Death

Jade crossed Michael's mind and although she and he shared his wife's pussy, in his heart he still couldn't get her out of his system. She was his crack and he was a junkie for her love.

When she died a piece of his heart died with her. One of his deepest regrets was that he was unable to have a part in his child's life. Jade made it known that she was not going to allow him an opportunity to be a father. Yes, he burned a bridge with Jade, but he would have given anything just to see his child's face. Now its 20 years later and the time had come and gone for him to be a father to the child he never knew.

For many years Michael and Roses lived with the thought of Jade getting revenge on them for what she felt was betrayal, but as the years went by nothing ever materialized, and they went on with business as usual.

Now that she was gone, Mike still thought of her daily. He prayed to God each night that his secrets were buried along with her. Although, he loved Jade, he made it known to her that he was not going to leave his home to set up shop with her. As for his marriage, he and Roses stayed together and raised their baby. They never spoke Jade's name again after they last saw her in 88.

Michael found out that Jade delivered his baby in the fall of 1988 from a mutual friend. Since the information was disclosed to him, he held on tighter to what he had at HOME with his wife. He had to say that his wife, Roses was a solider who was down for him; and she took her vows for better or for worse to heart.

The passing of Jade was a shock to the both of them. He did not attend the funeral but he did have a chance to see Jade about a month before she passed. She still looked good and after all those years he still wanted her.

They were both in Washington, DC on business. Michael bumped into her at the Reagan National Airport. When their eyes met, it was like a fire ignited. He walked over to her and started a conversation. "Jade, it's been a long time. Where are you headed?" He asked her as he grabbed her luggage. She gave him the most seductive look that made his man erect.

"Well what are you doing here without your beloved wife?" She said sarcastically.

"I'm here on business and you?" He responded.

"Just like you I'm here on business and possibly pleasure if you're game. I'm staying at the Renaissance hotel in NW, room 1610. You can stop by tomorrow night for old time sakes." She smoothly said as she entered the awaiting limo. She placed a room key in his hand and said, "I will be expecting your arrival."

Michael knew he had opened Pandora's Box again when he called her. He was starting to get the feeling that seeing Jade was not coincidental- to just happen to bump into your baby's mama after 20 years- the shit seemed to be scripted. But being the man he was, he just couldn't walk away. He was fienin for her. After Michael confirmed that Jade was in her room he called for the limo to pick him up and take him to the Renaissance Hotel.

Once at the hotel he took the elevator to the 16th floor and found his way to room 1610. He took a deep breath before he placed the key in the door. He could hear moaning and when he got inside his jaw dropped. There was more pussy in the room than he expected. What he saw was a beautiful Latina woman rubbing her shaved pussy on

Jade's clit and beautiful light skinned black woman sitting on Jade's face.

He stood watching the action for a few minutes. The three of them seemed oblivious to his presence. He sat in the nearest chair and played with his dick. He could feel the Viagra kicking in. His dick was rock hard and he was ready to jump into some pussy.

He made his way to the bed and placed his dick in the ass of the Latina girl. She tensed up from pressure of his dick, but loosened up and began to throw it back to him. He wanted to get his dick wet in all of the available pussy; so he moved the first girl to the side, and she and the black girl began to do the 69 on each other.

Michael submersed his python black dick into Jade's wet and awaiting pussy with the precision of an artist working on a masterpiece. She and Michael moved to a steady beat of a bass drum. Her goodies were better than he last remembered. After all this time her pussy was still tight and wet.

Her sugar walls gripped his dick and he immediately started to push his love in her faster and harder. He was in a state of intoxication. He was drowning in the abyss of her passion. He could feel his hot lava coming to a head and he erupted.

The four of them engaged in an orgy that lasted the entire weekend. They stayed in the suite until Monday morning. When they finally departed, and went their respective ways, a sense of sadness overcame Mike's body. It was like he was walking away from something that was truly precious to him. That very moment, he wondered what it would have been like if he had left Roses to be with Jade. He could not believe that after almost 20 years she still had this irreplaceable hold on him.

Now, looking back on the many choices he made, he wished he could change many of his actions. Mostly, Michael wished he could have been a better man to his wife and a better father to his child, but the hold Jade had on him was unmistakable.

He couldn't change the past; he could only move forward from this point on. Jade was his favorite girl and he would always miss her. She could never be replaced in his heart and mind. Mike wished he could have said goodbye to her on better terms. But life is for the living and that's what he planned to do.

Roses......3 Months After Jade's Death

Roses couldn't lie. She thought of Jade everyday. From the first time she was with her, she knew that she could not give up pussy. Jade was her first but not her last. Roses was devastated when she was told that Jade was no longer among the living. She cried for three days after she found out she was dead.

Roses still masturbated with the thoughts of them together. Jade exposed her to a new world of pleasure that was unknown to her. Before she was seduced by Jade, she never thought she would be a carpet muncher; but much to her surprise she loved it. Six months after Roses had her baby she started her quest for a new woman.

She had slept with several other women behind her husband's back since their last time with Jade. Roses was even brazen enough to bring one of her lovers in her home and into the bed she shared with Michael.

With all of the pussy she was getting, she was always looking for someone who was like or better than Jade. But, she came to the conclusion that she was never again in this lifetime going to find another like her-Jade was definitely a one of a kind.

As Roses reminisced on what could have been between she and Jade; she always waited for the day Jade was going to pay her back for her betrayal. Roses wanted to be with Jade, but she couldn't raise her child with another woman...how would that have looked? Today it's common for same-sex couples to have and raise children, but back in the day that shit was Taboo.

A little over a year ago she dreamed of Jade and in her dream she and Jade were together like old times. Her face and body were still as beautiful as she remembered. In her dream Jade told her that she still loved and dreamed of her often. Her dream seemed so real that she awoke in a cold sweat.

Two weeks later, she received a package. In the package was a black Armani suit and a Victoria Secret black cut-out teddy. The gifts put a smile on Roses face. She was sure they were from Mike, but when she opened the card she was shocked to find the package was from none other than the woman in her dreams.

The letter was sprayed with the sweet smell of Jade's favorite Jadore perfume. She inhaled the scent and read the letter:

To the Woman of my dreams,

I know it has been a long time. I know I'm the last person whom you would expect to hear from. Roses, I've been having the urge to see you again. I could feel in my spirit that I have crossed your mind. I would love to see you. I hope you will not reject my offer and answer my call.

Jade

There was a roundtrip ticket to Las Vegas for the next weekend and a room key to The Palms Erotic Suite. Roses was so shocked and surprised that she immediately cleared her schedule. In the process of preparing for the upcoming trip, it occurred to her, this trip was planned at the same time that Michael would be out of town with his brother. She was all too happy because she did not have to conjure up a lie in order to take the trip.

The week went by so slow that she was ready to leave for Vegas on Monday. Thursday finally came and Roses was ready to go. She arrived in "Sin City" and was taken in by the sights of the city. She went to the hotel and checked into the penthouse.

The penthouse was like nothing she had seen before. The suite, better yet, the apartment was both sensual and seductive. One could live out their wildest fantasies and fetishes and never feel out of place. The room was suggestive and catered to the sexual appetite. Roses was in her element and she was anticipating what was in store for her.

Once she got acclimated with her surroundings, she was ready to venture out and try her hand with lady luck. She showered and put on a little black dress with open toed stilettos. She took off her bridal set and placed it in the room safe. Roses went in her purse, pulled out the Zales box with the 2-carat ring from Jade, placed it on her ring finger, and proceeded out the door.

It was her first time in Las Vegas and she planned to live it up. Roses started off at the slot machines and won a few dollars, but after a few drinks she felt like playing a game that was more challenging. She walked over to the Blackjack table, sat down and ordered another Tequila Sunrise. She was feeling good and was actually winning. As the game progressed two women walked up to the table.

She paid them no attention, because by then she was inebriated. After several more hands, she, and the two women exchanged lustful looks. The women were beautiful and she could feel the heat emanating between her thighs. Her womanhood was throbbing. She was fantasizing about releasing her nectar down their tongues.

As they continued to exchange sex faces, the two women engaged in a kiss. The kiss was tantalizing. After witnessing such a provocative kiss, she could not stand it. Roses had to excuse herself from the game before her panties were wet and sticky from her juices.

She picked up her drink, winnings, and walked to the elevator. A hand was placed between the elevator's doors preventing their closure. In walked the ladies from the table. *Their eyes met simultaneously and there was no question as to what they were about to do.*

Roses walked over to them and they began to kiss and grope each other. They were insensate to the world. The ride to the penthouse was the pathway to her bondage and dominance sexual expedition. Once in the suite, she was tied up with the stockings of the mocha chocolate woman. After she was tied, both women went to work on giving her orgasms that were beyond her wildest capacity to imagine.

She was naked on the bed with her body spread eagle for them to devour as if she were their prey. Roses laid on the bed with a throbbing clit yearning for the touch of soft lips. Just when she thought she was going to explode from anticipation, she could feel one of them sucking her enlarged clit; while the other feverishly licked the inner walls between her thighs.

The pleasure she felt sent such a sensation through her body. She was overwhelmed with such sexual desire that she was having epileptic convulsions of orgasms.

Once the women came up for air from eating her pussy, she saw a familiar face, Jade. She squatted over Roses' face revealing a beautiful shaved pussy. Her mouth watered from the anticipation of the tasting of her.

Jade lowered her pussy to her face so her pussy and Roses' mouth could get acquainted. While she delivered her expert tongue action to her pussy, she could feel the other women fucking her with a double headed dildo. Roses stopped licking Jade as she released a moan of pure pleasure.

Jade grabbed the back of her head and raised it towards her clit. She rode her tongue until she squirted down her esophagus. Roses gladly swallowed Jade's cum and was instantly filled with satisfaction.

That was the night she indulged in unspeakable acts that she only thought was performed in porno movies. When she awoke from her love hangover Jade and the other woman was gone. There she was laying in the scent of sex; when she noticed a wig with a note attached beside the bed.

As she gathered her thoughts...thoughts of the previous night's sexapade brought a huge smile to her lips. She pulled herself from the bed and retrieved the note:

Roses,
I hope you enjoyed last night. Your pussy is still good to me after all these years. Enjoy the rest of your stay in Vegas.

Jade
XOXO

The rest of Roses' stay in Vegas was enjoyable. She saw a show, did more gambling, and yes, slept with another woman. But she never saw Jade again. Roses never spoke of her trip to Vegas to another soul. What goes on in Vegas stays in Vegas!!!

Now that Jade was gone she thought of that weekend often in her mind. Every time she had thoughts of her Vegas trip her juices flowed between her legs. How she longed to be with her again, but she was only with her in her mind.

Fourth of July Weekend…..The Present…Mikleah

The 4th of July weekend was approaching and Mikleah was preparing for the cookout at Ross' parents house. She was anxious for two reasons- it was her first time meeting her people and two they were going as a couple. Because, Ross was not open about her sexuality she was nervous about how her parents and family would take the fact that she preferred pussy to dick.

Mikleah assured her that her parents were not going to disown her. The cookout was on Saturday. She only had three days to find an outfit. Because Ross was not going to be free, she called Todd. Since he was headed to

Atlanta for business she decided to ride with him.

Todd and Kleah had been friends for so long that she often wondered what it would be like to be his woman. She never told Ross, but she loves dick just as much as she loves pussy. She never found a man who was able to give her sexual gratification.

The trip to Atlanta was just what she needed- a nice distraction from the drama in her life. She and Todd stayed at the downtown Marriott. Whenever she was with Todd, she never paid for anything. He always made sure she had what she wanted and needed; and he never pressured her for sex. For those reasons alone, she wanted him for herself; but she decided to give the relationship between Ross and herself a chance to work.

She was able to find a nice black Channel summer dress in Saks and some opened-toe stilettos. They returned from their trip on Friday and Mikleah was actually looking forward to the cookout. She made up her mind that she was going to enjoy her time with her baby and her people.

It was finally Saturday and Mikleah was excited. She was going to get her some free food, free liquor, and she was going to spend time with Ross. She started her day early because she had to get prepared for her outing.

She was feeling good and decided to soak in the tub

before she left the house. Mikleah started the water in the tub and went to turn on some music. Surprisingly she had some R&B in the CD player and not her normal hip hop/rap.

She soaked in the tub and the water felt good over her body. The smooth sounds of Anita Baker, Chaka Khan, Maze and Raheem Devaughn relaxed her mind and body.

She closed her eyes and imagined Todd in the tub with her. She could feel his soft dark skin on hers. With his LL Cool J lips caressing the nape of her neck. His touch was so real that she could feel his hands exploring her body. His masculine hands grabbed her breasts and teased them until they became erect. Once he was satisfied with the firmness of her nipples he ventured into her hidden cave.

He flicked his thumb over her clit while he inserted his index and middle fingers in and out of her passion. The foreplay he was giving her was driving her to the point of no return. As his fingers were working in and out of her, Mikleah began to move her hips to the rhythm of his movements. She exploded as she began to feel herself succumb to the orgasm that was erupting from within.

When she opened her eyes, she felt all the pent up frustration gone. The thoughts of Todd made her masturbating session worth it, but, now it was time to wash her ass and start the day.

By the time she got dressed and out the house it was 10:00. She had to get her hair, nails, and toes done so she was pressed for time. Luckily, everything would be a one stop trip. After a full day at the salon, Mikleah was looking to good. She ended up getting her hair in a bun ponytail with swept bangs. She wanted something simple but classy. It was already three in the afternoon by the time she got home.

Once at home she decided to call Todd and have him come over and smoke one with her. When Todd came over, they clowned and smoked. By the time it was time to meet Ross at her parent's house she was high as a kite. She was ready to get her eat and drink on. Mikleah pulled up to the house and could see the house was packed with people. She went to the door and rang the doorbell not knowing what to expect.

As she waited for the door to open she wondered how she was going to be received as Ross' girlfriend, just as her thoughts were getting deeper the door opened. "Hey you must be Ross' friend we've been waiting for you. I'm Ross' mother Ms. Jenks." She said as she gave her a hug and welcomed her into her home.

"Thank you for inviting me to the cookout and I'm glad to finally get the chance to meet you, Ms. Jenks." Mikleah said as she was escorted to the back yard where the rest of the guests were. As she looked around the crowd of people, Ross came up to her and gave her a hug and a kiss. *"What's up boo! I'm so glad that you are here. Let me introduce you to my father and some other people."* Ross told her as they headed over to some of the other guests.

As they approached a man that seemed to be Ross' father she looked at him as if she knew him from somewhere. For a man in his forties, he was still handsome and she could tell that back in the day he was a ladies man. But it was something about his eyes that memorized her; it was like she could see herself through them. As they approached him and the others, Mikleah pushed her feelings aside and continued to enjoy the evening.

After all of the formal introductions Ross and Mikleah started enjoying the evening. The drinks, food, and music was flowing, and the atmosphere was chill. People started to dance and play spades and dominoes; the night was going along well. The cookout was still going strong. Surprisingly enough, there were still plenty of people still at the house enjoying their 4th.

The party moved from the outside to the inside because the night's air brought a slight breeze. The night was going along well for Mikleah until she went to the bathroom. While she was in the bathroom handling her personal business she noticed that there was a box sitting on the countertop with her name written in black marker on the front.

At first, she thought her drunken ass was trippin, but as she got closer to the sink to wash her hands; she realized that the box was definitely addressed to her! Mikleah carefully examined the box before she picked it up. She made sure the door was locked and sat back on the toilet. She could feel the hairs on her arms standing up. She started to become afraid, because she wasn't sure if someone was stalking her, and followed her to the cookout or if the box was a gift from Ross.

She decided that she was going to find out one way or the other what was in that box. Mikleah began opening the box being careful not to destroy its contents. When she finally reached what was inside, her curiosity was peeked even more. The box only held a DVD with "PLAY ME" written on it. She looked at the writing to see if the print looked familiar. By this time whatever buzz she had was gone, because she sobered up quick!!!

She gathered the box, the DVD, and left for the living room. She went to find Ross and showed her the DVD. "Where did this come from?" Ross asked as she took the DVD out of her hands.

"I got it from the bathroom. It was there in this box with my name on it. I want to see what's on it." She said as she walked up to the television and turned it on so that the mysterious DVD could be played for all to see.

As Ross prepared to show the DVD, Mikleah could hear Ross making an announcement to the crowd that we were about to watch what was on the DVD. Ross' parents along with some of the other guests walked up closer so they could get a better view of the television.

There was a momentary silence as Ross grabbed the remote control and pushed play. When the DVD was played, all hell broke loose. What was displayed on the big screen shocked everybody. Mikleah was floored when she saw what was on the DVD. She was numb and all she could do was scream. Her heart was broken and her spirit was crushed beyond repair.

"What the fuck is this shit!!! Is that my mother?!" She screamed out. She could not believe her eyes. Mikleah was watching her mother fucking what looked to be both of Ross' parents. Ross' father was fucking her mother in the

ass while her mother fucked his wife with a dildo.

"Oh my God"! She heard Ross' mother scream as she quickly moved to turn off the entertainment and her husband hurriedly ushered the remaining guests out of the house. The embarrassment of his personal life was on display for all to see. The most humiliating thing of the situation was that his dirt was being revealed before the eyes of his daughter.

Once the house was cleared Ross, her parents, and Mikleah remained. The tension in that room was so thick that a knife could have sliced it. As they stood in total disbelief, Mikleah had the most shocking revelation; that the eyes of this man that stood before her were also her eyes; that the same blood that flowed through her veins flowed through his also.

She had to ask him, "What is your first name?" Although, she knew the answer, she needed confirmation.

He walked over to her and he could see that she was visibly shaken. When she looked into his eyes, Mikleah could see a reflection of herself. At that moment, her world was truly turned into a downward spiral.

"My name is Michael and yes many years ago I had an intimate relationship with Jade. I think it's possible that you could be my child." He said.

When he uttered those words, Mikleah was ready to explode, because this nigga was playing on her intelligence, and he had the balls to be condescending. Her words were sharp and to the point.

"You sorry motherfucker! How in your ever-loving life can you stand in my face and deny what you know to be the truth! The resemblance between us is undeniable! To add insult to injury, I've been fucking your daughter...my damn sister! Before you even part your mother-fucking lips to say anything about my mother, you better check yourself, because you and your wife were both fucking her, and had been doing so even after the both of you decided to call the affair off! Now stand in my face and call me a liar!" The realization of those words hit Mikleah like a ton of bricks, because she just confessed to doing the forbidden-committing incest with a woman who she had no idea was her family, but her sister.

Ross' mother walked up to her and said, "Look I know that you are hurt and in shock, but you will not come in my house, and speak to my husband in that manner or in the tone you are taking!"

Mikeah looked at her like she was crazy. She had some damn nerve when she had been doing the same thing as her husband and continued to do so after the relationship with her mother was over.

She knew it was time for her to leave before she caught a case. Before she left the house; Mikleah turned, looked into each of their eyes, grabbed her car keys, purse, and left. As she was walking to her car she could hear Ross calling out to her. As much as she wanted to go to her, she knew that part of her life was dead.

She could barely make it to the bathroom when she got home. Mikleah was so sick from the night's events that she vomited for at least fifteen minutes. After that ordeal she jumped in the shower. She felt so dirty.... she was mentally and spiritually filthy.

Kleah was trying to wash away all of the disgust, pain, and shame she felt away. The more she tried, the dirtier she felt. There was nothing she could do to change that feeling. She felt as if her life was all a lie and with that thought she could no longer contain the tears. She slid to the floor of the shower, pulled her knees to her chest, and cried until she could cry no more.

Ross was crushed. Her mind could not grasp the fact that the woman she had been sleeping with for the last year was her own flesh and blood. How could that be? Additionally, she had just seen her parents having a threesome with her sister's dead mother.

In Ross' mind, she needed an explanation as to why her world had just come undone around her. She went to her mother and looked at the woman who raised her, but all she saw was her getting fucked by another woman.

"What just happened here tonight? Please tell me it's all a big joke and the joke is on me!" Ross asked her mother with the sound of great despair in her voice.

The look on her mother's face spoke volumes. It became all to clear that everything Ross thought she knew about her parents had been a lie.

"Ross, I can't talk to you about this right now. All you need to know is that this is a personal matter between your father and I. We will handle this." Roses said.

Mike went to his daughter to comfort her. As he went to place his hands on his daughter, Ross immediately smacked his hand away.

"Don't you ever touch me again! Either one of you! I just found out that the both of you have been fucking the same woman, and that my father has an outside child; the girl that I have been fucking! And you feel I don't deserve an explanation for this shit! I can't believe I've been so blinded by all of your bullshit!" Ross yelled at both of her parents.

As Ross was venting all of her frustrations, Michel

had had enough of his daughter's tone and disrespect. He knew he had done wrong things in his life, but he would be damned if he would let a child of his disrespect him, especially in his own home.

As his daughter was speaking her peace, Mike raised his hand and slapped his daughter with such force that she fell to the floor. "I know you are upset by what you've seen, but don't you ever talk to me or your mother this way again in your life if you want to go on living! Right or wrong, we are still your parents and you will show us the respect we deserve! Do you understand?" He told his daughter as he stood over her.

Roses rushed to her daughter and helped her off the floor. "What the hell are you doing Mike? You cannot take your anger out on her when we are the ones who fucked up and brought this drama on ourselves." As Ross picked herself up from the floor, she looked at her parents with repulsion.

When she was able to compose herself, she gathered her things to leave. It was clear to her that she could no longer be in that house and look at her parents' faces.

"You know what, you're right, this is your house, and I will no longer be here. I'm out!" Ross said to her

parents as she walked out of the door to leave.

Her mother walked behind her not wanting her to leave. "Where are you going?" Her mother asked now shedding tears for a child that she had lost. Ross walked out the door never acknowledging her mother's words.

The Aftermath
Chapter 9

Roses

It had been 72 hours and Roses had fallen into a depression. She had taken an extended leave of absences from her job. Her life was in ruins and there was no one to blame, but herself. Michael was trying to keep it together, but underneath his manly exterior she knew he wanted to breakdown.

What hurt more was the fact that her child was gone and no one seemed to know where she was. How could she have known that her ghosts would come back in this way? While she was selling her soul for pleasure, she could not have imagined getting burned the way she did.

All she could do was sit and soak in her pain. Her family and friends tried to console her; the more they tried to comfort Roses the more she felt ashamed. If only she had known that her pain was only starting- there were more rainy days approaching.

Roses needed all of the strength she could muster. At night and frequently throughout the day she prayed to God: God grant me the serenity to accept the things I can not change. The courage to change the things I can and the wisdom to know the difference. Lord, forgive me of my sins, and help me to mend the broken pieces of my life. These blessings I ask in your son Jesus' name.

Roses' days were long, filled with despair, and she had no idea if her other sins were going to rear their ugly head again. She felt as if she was on the verge of a nervous breakdown. Roses always knew she was playing with fire, and one day, she knew she would get burned.

In a sordid way, she was relived, and in another sense; she was petrified. Whatever her feelings were, Roses was going to prepare for the worse and pray for the best.

This was the best and only thing she could do. It was hard to go on, but she had to be an adult and take responsibility for her actions...regardless of the consequences. Roses thought she was ready for whatever.

Michael

He could not believe his dirty secrets were coming into the light. Michael had never been more embarrassed in all his life. He was so busy doing his own thing that he never saw his downfall coming.

He was walking on eggshells at work, because he knew people had heard what had happened. Mike had worked so hard, was promoted swiftly, and now everything he had worked for was going down the drain.

Not only was his job that he had worked on for the last 20 years was in jeopardy; but he was forced to accept the fact that he had two daughters instead of one. Michael was having feelings of overwhelming guilt, because he was in Ross' life, but not Mikleah's life.

To add insult to injury, because they didn't know they were sisters, they had been fucking each other for over a year. He had never been faced with such adversity in his life. Now, he had to find a way to overcome it. His first priorities were to help Roses through her depression, find Ross, and lastly try to connect to the daughter he never knew he had.

It seemed as if he was living in a fucked up dream that he couldn't wake up from. Michael always knew in his heart that one day he would be exposed, but never in a million years; did he ever think it would be like this.

He was trying his best to keep his shit together, but it was hard. Michael was facing the fight of his life; and it was going to take everything within him to make it out of this without a scratch. He was preparing himself for anything, because something inside of him told him; that the shit was going to be worse, before the shit got better. Michael, knew this was not the end, but this was the beginning of his downfall. It was time to get his house in order before it was too late.

Although, he was going through a crisis in his life, he knew he had to make things right with his family; especially with Mikleah. Michael cancelled all of his appointments and spent the day in his office making phone calls.

Ross

Six weeks had passed since she last seen or spoken to her parents. Ross was still in the city but laying low. She was angry and confused by the recent turn of events that occurred in her life. The only person who Ross had contact with was her grandmother, her mom's mother. She had gone to her for comfort and advice. Her grandmother was the one person she felt safe with. Everyone else in Ross' life had turned into her enemy.

Although, her grandmother did not approve of her parent's actions, she encouraged Ross to see her mother. Her grandmother informed her that her mother had fallen into a state of depression. Although, her grandmother informed her of her mother's condition, she was still not ready to face her.

Her grandmother was the peace maker and she took

it upon herself to heal the pieces of her broken family. It was the third weekend in August when her grandmother summoned all of them to her house for a family get together. They were all gathered at the house, and the tension was thick. This was the first time since the 4th of July that Ross had seen her parents.

Ross remembered her mother coming to hug her, but she rejected her. She couldn't understand why she was so mad with her mother, but not with her father. They had both engaged in the same act, - threesome. As much as she was hurt by their actions; she had to respect the fact that they were still her parents.

"Rosslyn, I am so sorry for the pain that I have caused you. I never meant to hurt you. You are my child and I would lay down my life for you. I love you more than life itself." Roses said to her daughter in an attempt to reconcile.

Her words pierced Ross' soul. Although, her past transgressions came to light; by all accounts she had been a good mother to her.

Ross was speechless and could not respond to her words. Her mother embraced Ross and they cried together. Her tears were a release of all the feelings that were embedded in her mind, body, and spirit.

As they stood in the middle of the living room having their moment, her father came to join them, and the three of them hugged for what seemed to be an eternity.

Ross was feeling better, because she had made peace with her parents and the night was going fine. The family was together and the tension dissipated. They ate a good home cooked meal prepared by yours truly, Ross' granny. It had seemed like ages since all of her immediate family was together-her parents, her aunts, her dad's brother and wife along with all of her cousins.

After dinner, they decided to play board games, spades, and the PS3. The music was loud as hell, and all who were able to drink were getting their drink on. The party was just getting started. Her father and uncle wanted to embraced their inner child and play each other in a game of Madden.

As they played the video game they all gathered around the big screen to watch them battle with their favorite football teams. They were all chilling and enjoying the relaxed atmosphere when the game seemed to mal-function, and the big screen seemed to get fuzzy like when a television station goes off the air.

It seemed like Ross was caught in the Matrix.....she was physically there, but the events around her were surreal. The game was now gone, and the 56-inch screen television was now showing once again a familiar face. There she was once again for all to see; but this time instead of a porno show of Jade; the screen was leaking buried secrets of others.

Ross suddenly snapped back to reality when she heard the screams bellowing from her grandmother and mother. Although, she was unaware of what she was saying, she saw the affect of her words.

There was chaos in the house. She was glued to her seat. She was in a dream and the only thing Ross remembered was the sound of gunshots. The room became silent and the only sound
that was heard was the moans of life leaving someone's body. Her father raised his body from atop of Ross' and they stood up.

The unimaginable had happened. Her granny was standing over her mother and her husband still holding his gun in her hands. Her mother and step-grandfather were lying in a pool of blood on the floor.

"Oh my God! What have you done granny!!! Give me the gun!" Ross said as she inched her way over to her grandmother. There was a look in her granny's eyes that she never in her life seen before. It was as if she was in a

trance and having an out of body experience.

She approached her as calmly as she could. Ross gently grabbed her hand taking the gun. As soon as she had the gun in her hand, her uncle grabbed it from her.

Her grandmother looked at her and shook her head. "Why is your mother and grandfather on the floor bleeding?" Her grandmother said as she bent down attempting to hold them in her arms. Although, Ross was terrified, she could not give that impression. She needed to be strong and take control of the situation. Ross was trying to access the situation while her father held her mother in his arms crying. This was the first time Ross had seen him cry.

Her aunt dialed 911, and her uncle and cousins stood outside the house waving the ambulance and police down as they sped down the street to the house. Ross was able to get her granny to sit down on the couch as she went over to her mother and grandfather. She grabbed her mother's hand as her tears began to flow. Between sobs, her father told her to check on her grandfather.

When Ross turned and grabbed his hand, she knew he was dead. After feeling his lifeless hand, she yelled out in grief.

"My God! He's dead!!! He's dead!! Granny why

would you do this, poppa loved you!" She yelled in grief.

Granny was sitting on the couch rocking back and forward humming the words to What a Friend We Have in Jesus. The police and the paramedics came rushing in asking them to move so they could attempt to save her mother. They all stood by as they went to work on her. There was not a dry eye in the room. The paramedics hurriedly put Roses in the ambulance and rushed her to the hospital.

As they prepared to leave for the hospital, the police were placing Ross' granny in handcuffs and leading her to the awaiting police car. When they stepped out of the house, the street was filled with concerned people from the neighborhood. The look on the neighbor's faces showed their shock and surprise.

Ross' grandparents were well known in the African-American community and to all looking from the outside in, they were upstanding, law abiding, Christian people.

While she and her father were at the hospital, her Uncle Keith went to the police station to be with her granny while she waited for her attorney. He would make sure she didn't say anything without the presence of her attorney. Aunt Sade took the children home and told them she would be at the hospital as soon as she found a babysitter.

Ross was always afraid of hospitals and never had any desire to enter one unless it was life or death. Her nerves were shot and she needed a shot of Patron. What she also wanted was for Mikleah to be there with her. She was scared and wanted her there for support.

She was so confused, because although she knew they were sisters she still wanted her sexually; but Ross knew that shit could never happen again. Yet, at that moment, she wanted her to be there for her and their father.

She had built up the nerve to pick up her cell phone and dial her number. Ross was nervous, because it had been over a month since she and Mikleah had spoken or seen each other.

Her mind was racing. She was afraid Mikleah was going to ignore her and not answer the phone. The phone rang until the voicemail picked up. As soon as she heard her voice, she broke down sobbing. She was able to compose herself enough to leave a message. Ross pleaded for her to come to the hospital.

The only thing she could do now was wait for information on her mother and wait in vain for Mikleah to get back to her. She didn't know what was worse, waiting in vain for Mikleah or waiting for the possible impending death of her mother.

It had been hours and the doctor still hadn't come in to give them an update on her mother's condition. As they waited, the hospital morgue informed them that someone needed to identify her grandfather's body.

Michael and Ross went into the cold room where his body was laying stiffly on the table. When the sheet was pulled back from his body, she began to cry, because she couldn't understand how a man who she loved just as much as her own father ended up dying at the hands of his own wife- her granny.

Ross was so drained after identifying her grandfather's body she felt as if she had nothing else to give. Her heart was heavy and her family link had been broken. Her life was fucked up and she just knew it wasn't going to get better anytime soon.

72 hours had passed and her mother was still in the ICU. The doctor advised them that she would make a full recovery, but it was unknown how long she would be in her comma.

Dr. Muhammad came to them and said, "Mr. Jenks and Rosslyn your wife/mother will be fine. Her brain is functioning normally and from all the tests that were run on her it appears that no permanent damage was detected.

However, because she experienced a traumatic injury, her body must get over the shock that occurred to her. Therefore, Mrs. Jenks will be in her comma until her mind and body is able to get over the stress of the accident." He told them.

Ross and her father looked at each other. They were extremely grateful that she was going to be alright, but they were worried about her being in a self-induced coma. The news from Dr. Muhammad was bittersweet. They knew she would be fine, but it would be a matter of time before she would come back to world.

Granny was well off in her old age therefore, she had the monetary funds to retain one of the top criminal defense lawyers in the state. Her attorney Jeremiah Blackwell was known for getting the well to do people and the infamous drug dealers acquitted. He was able to get her released on $300,000 bail under the condition that she was released to the custody of the family.

Granny was still not herself after she was released from jail. She showed little emotion and she went on as if nothing had happened. Because her house was still considered a crime scene, she was living at Michael and Roses' house.

Ross took her to see her mother in the hospital, but

she had no recollection of what transpired. She went on as if her daughter's accident was a random act of violence committed by an unknown perpetrator. Ross was so concerned about her mental health that she conferred with her attorney about getting her to a psychologist.

They were able to get her to see a recommended psychologist so she could get properly diagnosed with what was going on in her head. All was well in Ross' life until now. She had become a sad, lonely, and devastatingly dysfunctional person.

Her grandfather had been dead for little over a week and the funeral was scheduled for Saturday. Her grandfather's family was coming to town from all over. She and her father made all of the arrangements while her grandmother wrapped her mind around the unbelievable- the death of her husband.

He outlived his siblings, but their children, and grandchildren were in attendance at the funeral. The funeral was so packed with people. Some were family and friends while others were nosey individuals trying to get the scoop on the family tragedy.

There were so many rumors going around in the streets. Like her granny killed her grandpa for his money and that she walked in on him sleeping with his long-time mistress. The rumors were endless. Needless to say the funeral was a spectacle for all to see.

Guilt or Innocence
Chapter 10

The charges against Ross's granny were one count of first degree murder and one count of attempted murder. Her attorney, Mr. Blackwell, was able to get the trial delayed for three months.

The trial was set to begin in November. The months leading up to the trial were trying times for the entire family. Roses was still in the ICU in a comma, Michael was trying to hold it together, Ross' granny would never be the same again, and Ross was trying to be the glue that kept the family together.

Ross felt drained and alone...she needed someone she could lean on. The only person she wanted to bear her soul to was Mikleah. It had been months since she had left the message for her. Now, Ross was going to pay her a visit.

The trial was to begin in early November and she decided to pay her sister a visit the Saturday before the trial. She was extremely nervous and anxious. Things in her life were an up and down everyday struggle and she needed a stable fixture in her life.

The 15 minute drive to her house seemed like hours.

As she made her way to the other side of town, all of her thoughts were on how she would be received by Mikleah. It had been months since they had seen each other. The last time they were together they found out that they were the fucking incest sisters.

As she pulled onto Mikleah's street, she could see her car parked in the driveway. Ross parked her car and slowly emerged from the car to face her fears. When she got to the door and before she could ring the doorbell, Mikleah opened the door to let her in the house.

They walked to the living room in silence. They sat there for several minutes until Ross could not contain her emotions any longer. She began to cry hysterically. All of the pain she had been holding in was coming out.

Mikleah came over to Ross and held her in her arms as she released all of the frustration that she had buried in her soul. She cried for what seemed like an eternity. After, she could not cry anymore, Mikleah looked at her with such compassion in her eyes and said, "Look, Ross we were both shocked to find out that our relationship was built on deception. Now it's the time for us to make a mends between us, because we are family. I'm sorry things could not be the way we both envisioned, but from here on out we can redefine our relationship as sisters."

Her words were all the comfort Ross needed. Right then Ross knew she had someone who had her back. She had someone who was in her corner. Mikleah and Ross sat in the living room for hours talking. Ross told her about the shooting and how her grandfather died at the hands of her granny, and that her mother was in a self induced comma.

Mikleah agreed to go to the trial with her. She also agreed that she would attempt to get to know the father whom she never had the opportunity to know. She felt better when she left her house and her sprits were lifted. In Ross' heart and mind, she knew things were going to work out for the best. They just had too.

Mikleah

It's funny how someone who knows you well can always tell that you have them on your mind. Mikleah had been thinking about Ross lately and she felt as if she was thinking of her too; then today she appeared at her doorstep.

It was good to see Ross. Mikleah was hurt and disgruntle when the truth was revealed to her about whom she was, and whom she was screwing. She didn't know how to handle the situation.

In her mind, the best way to handle the situation

was for her to stay away. As much as she wanted to reach out to Ross and her so-called father, she just couldn't do it.

They say time will heal of all wounds. Although, she would never forget what had happened to her; she had to forgive in order to move on with her life. She had fallen into a depression and continued to blame herself for getting involved with her own sister; but how was she to know they were being incestuous. Nana and her aunt Jaylyn where trying their best to guide her through this dark period, but she couldn't find any closure.

She read and re-read her mother's diary searching for clues but there were none. Now, she had the chance to redeem her soul by trying to be there for her sister and getting to know the father she never knew she had. The more she thought about things, she knew her mother's revenge plot wasn't over.

Her mother was a woman who planned shit down to a "T" and she never left anything to chance. She already shamed Ross, and her mother, but she had yet to shame her father. Mikleah needed to know what her intentions were for him. She needed to defuse the situation before someone else was killed or placed behind the penitentiary bars.

The Trial
Chapter 11

"Ladies and Gentlemen of the jury I will show beyond a shadow of a reasonable doubt that my client, Ms. Lena Williamson is not guilty of murder. The only crime she is guilty of is defending a bruised and battered heart. It is my job to provide the best defense for Ms. Williamson and there will be evidence presented to this wonderful jury that will prove her innocence. The only remedy to this tragic situation is a not guilty verdict." The opening statement of Lena's attorney was off the chain. He had all the jurors eating out of the palm of his hands, not to mention he was delicious eye candy to look at.

Lena's attorney had advised her to plead not guilty to the two counts she was charged with on the grounds of temporary insanity. He was confident that his client would be vindicated and would not have to serve jail time. He was even more convinced that once the truth came out that she would have the sympathy of the public and the jurors.

The courtroom was packed. The publicity from the media made the case the most anticipated case in a while. Everyone wanted to know why she had snapped and killed her husband and almost killed her daughter in the process. The streets were talking and the rumors were flying.

Everybody was speculating, but no one really knew the truth.

Lena sat in the defendant's chair wearing a Versace black suit, her face was perfectly made, and a fresh hair-do straight from the salon. Her demeanor was one of complete self-assurance. The prosecution was ready to present their argument to all who were ready to hear, but no one really gives a fuck about the guilt or innocence of the accused. All anyone who is involved with a legal battle wants to know is which side can persuade the jury with the most bullshit.

The DA thought he had an open and shut case against Lena. It was true the evidence was damning, but her attorney was a vicious bit bull in an Armani suit. He also had some tricks up his sleeves as well.

The trial had been going on for the last three weeks and the DA was resting his case. Lena's attorney, Mr. Blackwell, was denied the opportunity to defend his client, because the judge ordered the court in recess until after the Thanksgiving holiday. The holidays were supposed to be for family, but this year the family was anything but together. Because of the family turmoil, they decided to have Thanksgiving dinner in a neutral location, at Miklelah's house. Since Roses was unable to be with them to give thanks to the Lord for all of His blessings, as a way to be inclusive, they made arrangements with the hospital to have a small dinner in her private room.

Michael, Ross, and Miklelah were making the best out of their current circumstances and realized that they were one...that they shared the same blood line, and they needed each other in order to get through the hard times. They collectively decided that they would go to the hospital the Wednesday before Thanksgiving and eat dinner with Roses.

Roses was in her hospital bed looking peaceful but very much in a coma. Michael and Ross both took turns talking to her and holding her hand; but she still wasn't ready to come out of her comatose state.

It was a nice feeling to have a father and a sister that Mikleah never knew she had with her. They ate and talked while they visited Roses. The feeling between them was one of optimism, but deep down Mikleah wanted to cry, because she secretly missed her mother. She was also sad to see Ross' mother in the condition she was in.

Mikleah and Ross prepared Thanksgiving dinner. The menu consisted of turkey, ham, macaroni and cheese, potato salad, squash, greens cornbread and a host of deserts. They had a lot of food to prepare. As soon as they left the hospital, the two sisters went to Mikleah's house to start their quest to feed the guests.

The time they spent together gave them the opportunity to get to know each other. They found out that it was not going to be as bad as they both thought it would be to be sisters. They talked about everything that was on their minds. Mikleah's curiosity was killing her because she was secretly jealous. Ross was able to grow up with a father and she wanted to know what it was like.

"Ross, what was it like to grow up with Michael as your father?" She asked her as she cleaned the collard greens. Ross took a moment and contemplated her question before answering.

"What do you what to know? I mean I could go on and on about how I grew up in a two parent household, but I thought I had given you a glimpse into my childhood once before. I will say, he definitely spoiled me and I'm definitely a daddy's girl. Although, my parents had many trying times in their marriage, he always sheltered me from their drama." Ross said.

She listened to every word Ross said and wondered to herself, was it too late to get that father-daughter bond with him. Although, her childhood was a good one; she always had an empty void, because of the absence of her father. But to give him some credit-she was quite sure that he would have taken responsibility for her if he had been given the time and opportunity.

Thanksgiving dinner at the house was civil to say the least and although, Mikleah was the new comer to this newly blended family; Michael made it known to everyone that she was apart of the family and no one was to disrespect her.

The food was good and all of them were on their best behavior trying hard not to bring up any current touchy situations. After dinner was served, things began to become more relaxed. The evening turned out to be an alright evening.

Ross and Michael stayed behind to help with the clean up and to have a recap of the night's events. Mikleah's emotions were on a rollercoaster, because she felt a sense of guilt. The confusion and turmoil was a direct cause of her deceased mother.

Mikleah tried to suppress those thoughts and continue on as if it was all good, but it was like her dead mother's spirit was coming to her and was trying to tell her something. Her presence was just too close to her spirit.

It was now time for the rumble in the courtroom. The prosecution had rested and now the time had come for Jeremiah to unleash his fury. Lena and Mr. Blackwell entered the courtroom ready for war. Lena looked stunning as usual, but the look in her eyes said something else. Mikleah was always told that the eyes were the key to the soul and she guessed Lena's soul was crying out.

Jeremiah had been going over the case with his client and everyone who was in the house at the time of the shooting. He went over the questions he was going to ask them and how they should respond to them. Although, Lena had committed the crime, no one in the family wanted her to serve any jail time. Now, it was time for her to fight like she was going down for the count.

The family and character witnesses were testifying the rest of the week. Lena was scheduled to take the stand the day after her psychologist Dr. Roman was done giving his professional medial opinion on Lena's mental state of mind. The court was adjourned for the day and Jeremiah wanted to go over the questions he had prepared for Lena's testimony.

"Listen Lena the trial is going in our favor. I was able to poke holes in the DA's witnesses. Also, testimonies from your family and friends have helped to shape a positive overview of you. Additional, Dr. Roman has given his medical opinion that at the time of the shooting you were temporarily insane and you exhibit signs of mental

instability. So, what I need you to do tomorrow is to be yourself and to tell the jury in your own words what happened." Jeremiah said as he sat across from her while they ate lunch.

Lena listened intently to every word. She was ready for whatever her fate was going to be. She missed her husband and was too ashamed to go see her daughter in the hospital. While in her counseling session with Dr. Roman, she was able to talk freely about her feelings about what she had done. It was not until recently that she asked for the Lord's forgiveness. Now she needed to make her peace with her daughter and her husband.

Lena had the rest of the day free and asked if Ross and Mikleah would carry her on errands to see Roses and her husband's grave. The three of them spent the remainder of the day together.

They shopped and just enjoyed themselves. They arrived at General Memorial Hospital around four in the afternoon.

"Ross and Mikleah thank you both for bringing me here. But, I need to speak my peace to Roses in private." Lena walked in Roses' private room closing the door behind her.

Lena was in the room with her daughter for the

better part of an hour. They sat there awaiting her return. Ross and Mikleah talked and that's when Mikleah confided in Ross that she thought something was wrong with her grandmother.

"Ross, I know Lena is your grandmother and I know you know her better than me. But, I think something's going on in her head." She told her, but, before Ross could respond Lena walked out of Roses' room.

They had small talk as they rode to the cemetery and they never questioned Lena about her visit with Roses. When they arrived at Mr. Williamson's place of rest, Lena got out of the car leaving them behind once again. This time, Ross and Mikleah sat in the car in silence and waited.

The Star Witness
Chapter 12

The prosecution had presented an excellent case based on forensic evidence but they had no motive. Attorney Blackwell had cross-examined all of the DA's witnesses and was able to raise reasonable doubt to the jury; but now it was time for his star witness- the accused herself.

10:00 am on Wednesday morning they walked in the courtroom dressed to the "T" with their heads held high. Ross, Michael, and Mikleah sat in the first row directly behind Lena and her defense team. Mr. Blackwell was prepared and Lena looked as if she was ready too. Dr. Roman finished his testimony from the day before and Lena took the stand to tell her side of the story.

"Do you have any more witnesses that you would like to call to the stand Mr. Blackwell"? The judge asked.

"Yes, your honor. I would like to call to the stand Mrs. Lena Williamson." Mr. Blackwell responded as he walked over to Lena and led her to the witness stand. As she walked to the stand, Ross and her sister held hands and waited for the outcome. She placed her right hand on the Bible and was sworn to tell the truth, the whole truth, and

nothing but the truth.

"Can you please state your name and current address for the record." Her attorney asked.

The courtroom was waiting with anticipation as they held on to her every word.

"Yes, my name is Lena Williamson and I reside at 1513 Cornell Blvd." She said as she looked directly at the 12 people who were going to decide her fate.

"Mrs. Williamson I'm going to ask you a few questions, ok. Can you please tell us to the best of your recollection the events that transpired on the 15th of August of this year?" Jeremiah asked.

Lena looked out in the crowd locking eyes with her grand-daughter and started her story.

"Well, I had invited everyone to my house for a small family get together. You see, my family had been going through some difficult times and being that I hate for my family to be at odds with each other, I wanted to make things right." Her story started off slow and calm. Before she continued on with the story, she asked for a glass of water.

"Please, Mrs. Williamson, take your time." Mr. Blackwell said to her as he patted her on the hand. Lena closed her eyes as if she was saying a mental prayer and

continued with her testimony.

"Well, I had cooked a big home cooked meal and we all had finished eating, so we decided to play some cards and other games for entertainment. My memory is a little sketchy after that." Lena said.

"Mrs. Williamson, I understand that this is traumatic, but I need you to try and remember all you can." Attorney Blackwell advised his client. He went back to the witness stand and offered her another slip of water.

"All I remember is that my son-in-law and his brother were sitting in front of our television set about to play a game and the next thing I know, Roses and Henry were laying on the floor bleeding and everyone was yelling, screaming, and crying." Her voice was low but understandable.

As Lena's testimony was coming to the part of the shooting of her daughter and husband, Ross began to sob uncontrollably and Michael held her in his arms to give her some comfort.

"So let me understand. You have no memory of the shooting of your husband and daughter- is that correct?" Mr. Blackwell asked as a man was rolling in a big screen television. Lena looked at her lap and rubbed her hands together then replied, "No."

"Judge, I would like to introduce this DVD into evidence labeled as exhibit AB. So just for the record Mrs. Williamson you have no idea as to why you snapped and shot both your husband and daughter?" He said.

"No, Mr. Blackwell I do not. My daughter and I have a wonderful relationship and my husband and I were happy for many years. Henry was the only father that Roses knew and the only grandfather to my grandbaby. I would never want to hurt either of them." Lena was visibly upset and shaken by the force of her attorney's questioning. Her tears pierced the flawless MAC make-up on her face.

"Members of the jury, I would like each of you to view this video, because it explains why my client is not guilty of murder. She is only guilty of not knowing how to deal with an acute family situation. Ask yourself members of the jury, what would your reaction be if you were placed in this situation?"

With those words, Jeremiah, pushed play on the DVD player and the truth was shown for all to see. Roses and her stepfather fucking!! He was fucking her from behind and it looked as if she was enjoying every moment of him pumping his manhood into her from the back.

The look on everyone's face including Mikleah's was one of disbelief and shock. How could they do this to someone they claimed to love? As all eyes were on the pornographic display, Lena was on the stand crying hysterically, speaking to Jesus asking for His forgiveness. Because all eyes were magnified to the 52 inch big screen television, no one saw Lena as she got up from the witness stand and pulled out the same gun that she used to kill her husband and shoot her daughter with.

As she pointed the gun to the temple of her head the bailiff yelled for her to drop her weapon as he reached and pulled his pistol from his holster. Immediately, all eyes were directed back at Lena. She walked from the stand and stood in the center of the room, all the while she was screaming that she was sorry for what she had done and that she loved her family.

Her attorney began to plead with her to put the gun down. "Jeremiah, do not come any closer to me!" Lena shouted. The court was in total confusion. Some people were running for the door while others like the media who were covering the trial stayed.

Ross stood up and yelled, "Granny please don't do this. We all love you!" As the bailiff moved in to take her down, Lena looked at Ross and said, "Ross I love you so much. My family was all that I had to live for and now my family can't be repaired. I'm so sorry for all that I have *done- Lord...take me now!!!" With those being her last words Lena pulled the trigger and released a 9-millieter slug into the dome of her head.*

Blood and her brain matter were spattered over the floor. It seemed to happen in slow motion, like they were watching a movie and it kept pausing and then replaying it's self live.

Suicide in the Courtroom
Chapter 13

Lena was lying in the middle of the courtroom with the top of her head blown away. Ross was in a state of frantic panic. She had just witnessed, along with hundreds of others, her grandmother commit suicide with a nine-millimeter. Her first instinct was to run to her grandmother's side, but Michael stopped her from going to see the grotesque sight.

"Granny. OH my God. Granny!!! Please God don't let her be dead!!!" This was all that Ross could bring herself to say. Mikleah held her sister and they both cried. "The two of you stay here!" Michael commanded them as he ran across the room to where Lena was laying in a pool of her own brains and blood.

The entire courtroom was in a frenzy. The EMS workers came rushing in trying to find the slightest sign of life left in her, but to no avail. Lena was gone before her body hit the floor.

The police were trying to restore order in the center of an extreme chaotic mess. The media was having a field-day with the events as they unfolded. Mikleah felt as if she was about to have a panic attack, but she knew she had to stay calm. She needed to be strong for Rosslyn. Her sister needed her right now and she needed to be there for her.

Everything happened in less than 10 minutes but it seemed like an eternity. As Michael was tending to Lena, Mr. Blackwell came and escorted them out of the room. His suit was soiled with blood and he was visibly shaken. As they were rushed from the courtroom, they were swarmed by the media. The police shielded them as they were led into an undisclosed location inside the courthouse.

Breaking News
Chapter 14

Roses awakened from her coma at the exact time her mother's body hit the cold floor of the courtroom. The medical staff quickly went to her room and began examining her. Dr. Muhammad was so glad to see her wake up from her self-induced comma.

"Welcome back to the world Roses!! You were gone for a while, but I am so happy to see you back among us and in good health." Dr. Muhammad said as he held her hand.

Roses was conscious and confused as to why none of her family was in the room with her.

"Where is everyone? How long have I been in here...in the hospital?" These were the first words Roses had uttered in the past three months.

Dr. Muhammad looked at his patient and admired her beauty. She was more concerned about her family verses the welfare of herself.

"Ms. Jenks you have gone through a traumatic experience. I want you to relax. You will be fine and have a speedy recovery. Your family will be notified about you being awake. I will be back to check on you later." Dr.

Muhammad said to her as he released her hand.

Roses was left alone in her room as the staff went to see other patients. She was left alone with her thoughts and the sounds of the television. She had been awake for less than 20 minutes when she saw the local television anchor chime in on the television with breaking news. Roses adjusted the back of her hospital bed and turned the volume up.

"Good afternoon, we have just gotten word from a confirmed source that there has been a shooting in the courthouse. Our source has told us at KWTA that a woman who was on trial for murder and attempted murder committed suicide while she was in the middle of testifying in her defense. Now, we will go live to the courtroom where Michele Justice is reporting." The anchor said as the news broadcast showed a live shot of the chaos outside of courtroom.

For some strange reason, Roses had an eerie feeling in the pit of her stomach. Her mind flashed back to the previous day when her mother came in to see her. Although, she was unconscious her brain was able to process what was going on around her. She was unable to speak to her mother, but she could definitely understand. Roses reflected back on what she had heard her mother say:

"Roses, I'm so sorry for what I have done to you. I don't know why I went to the extreme and decided to take things into my own hands instead of letting the Lord mend the broken fences. I don't know what made Henry and you sleep together and hurt me so. As much, as I want to blame him for the acts that the two of you committed- I can't, because that DVD showed you as a grown ass woman and not a minor. You knew exactly what you were doing!!

Now, I have made it so that we as a family can never get through this hardship. Roses, I just want you to know that my love for you is unconditional. I have forgiven you and I hope you can find it in your heart to forgive me for what I've done to you. I love you Roses- don't ever forget that and never let anyone tell you anything differently."

Roses remembered her mother's words and felt ashamed for what she had done with the only man she knew as her father.   The two of them never had a sexual relationship until she was 18. They always flirted when her mother wasn't around and he would masturbate her until she came and came again, but they never consummated the relationship until she was of legal consent.

Her step-father was her first lover. The both of them

were connected in a way that could not be described. The relationship continued until and during her marriage to Michael. Roses never expected her secret to be aired to the world. Now in retrospect she wondered how she allowed herself to be taped on numerous occasions. It was too late to reminisce and ask why- that shit was for the birds.

"Yes, today Mrs. Lena Williamson, age 60 killed herself in front of a courtroom filled to capacity with spectators. She was on trial for the murder of her husband and the attempted murder of her daughter." The reporter stated.

Roses heard the anchor say her mother's name but she couldn't understand what was said afterward. Her ears heard that she was dead, but her mind, body, and soul could not process the words. Roses' entire body was numb and she was confused.

Roses closed her eyes. When she opened them, she saw her mother standing in front of her. The image was so real to her that she gathered her strength and placed her feet on the floor. Once she was able to stand she began to walk toward her mother's figure and fell to her knees only to have her arms feel the cold air.

When she realized that her mind was conjuring her mother before her, she became overwhelmed with grief and heartache. The screams and wails that came from the room caused the nurses to come rushing into the room. The nurses found her on the floor screaming uncontrollably.

The nurses were perplexed by what was making her hysterical. It wasn't until one of the nurses noticed that her mother's face was flashing across the television with the caption under the picture saying that she was dead.

"Oh my God! Her mother killed herself!!!" One of the nurses said as she helped her colleague get Roses back in her bed. Dr. Muhammad was immediately paged to her room.

Dr. Muhammad came rushing in and asked no questions but proceeded to inject her with a sedative. Roses cried for a minute longer until the medication kicked in. Her eyes got heavier and heavier until she was finally asleep.

Dr. Muhammad placed Roses on a 24- hour suicide watch. Before he left her room, he sat in the chair next to her bed and held her hand.

"Roses, I know that you have been going through so much shit and you are mentally and physically tired. But, I need you to be strong. Whenever, I see you, you make my whole day brighter. I know that you are still married, but I want to make you my wife. I want you to have my child.

Baby, get better for me and I will be right here waiting for you." Dr. Muhammad confessed his feelings for a woman who he had fallen in love with.

He wanted her and he was not going to let anything get in the way of his goal. Dr. Muhammad was married, but he found out that his wife had gone outside of their marriage and found comfort in the arms of another woman.

When he found out about the affair he was distraught, but once he got over his pity party he told his wife that she could do her and he would do him. Now, that he was ready to leave, he felt he had found the one he wanted to continue his life with.

Nothing will be the Same Again
Chapter 15

Jeremiah, Ross, and Mikleah had been in a secluded room for little over an hour. Ross was still in shock and had not said a word. She sat in her chair with a blank stare on her face. Mikleah knew in her heart that she was gone. Ross was only an outer shell of herself. She walked over to Jeremiah and placed her hand on his shoulder.

"Are you alright? Do you need anything?" Kleah asked him as she sat next to him.

He turned to her and looked at her with piercing hazel eyes.

"No, boo I'm ok right now. We need to get your father and get the hell up out of here. I'm going call my people and get them out here to get us." Was his reply as he stood up and dialed the number on his cell.

She was mesmerized by his whole persona. She felt the chemistry between them from the first time they met, but she knew this was not the time for her to act on her sexual attraction towards him.

Mikleah walked over to Ross and tried talking to her again but she was not responding. She was in an emotional whirlwind. Mikleah wanted, in fact she needed, everything to be ok. She held Ross in her arms and rocked her back and forward. That was the only comfort she could give her sister.

Finally, Michael came to the room where they were. There were no words said only a mutual understanding between them. Kleah grabbed her purse and helped Ross to her feet. The four of them along with a police escort started for the front entrance of the courthouse. They were no less than 100 feet from the door when they could see the media circus on the outside. Jeremiah instructed Michael and Mikleah not to say a word and to keep moving toward the awaiting car.

They had made it outside the courthouse doors and the media was all over them. The questions kept coming from every direction but they kept it moving. Before they could make it to the car, a woman with her small entourage emerged from the crowd and blocked them from entering the Navigator. Her face looked familiar but Mikleah could not place her face.

The woman called Michael by his entire government name and said, "I represent the family of James and Tabitha Jackson. You have been served with legal documents claiming that you have had a sexual relationship with their minor daughter."

Jeremiah stepped in front of the woman and grabbed the paperwork.

"I will be representing Mr. Jenks and he will voluntarily come in for any questions at a later time." They pushed by the woman and her people and got in the SUV heading to Mikleah's house. They rode in silence. Each of them was in their own thoughts.

The sight of the woman who served Michael had Kleah searching her mind for where she knew her from. Then it hit her! That was Angela Martinez her mother's attorney. She knew the shit was about to go down and it was not going to be good. They arrived at her house and she immediately tended to her sister. She got her undressed and ran her a hot bubble bath.

When she got her in the tub she went into her room to get clothes that Todd had left to give to Jeremiah.

"You still have on these bloody clothes. Why don't you go to the bathroom take a shower and change." She said to him as she handed him the clothes. He graciously took them and headed to the bathroom to freshen up. Michael and Mikleah were left in the living room.

She went over to the bar to pour them both a shot of Patron.

"Look, Michael I understand that the last couple of

months have been understandably trying and confusing for you. I'm truly sorry for all of the drama that you have been through, but, now, we have to get past our issues, work together to get you out of this mess, and make sure that Ross is ok." She said as they finished their shots.

The father she never knew looked at her with eyes that were the same as hers and said, "Mikleah, I am sorry that I was not able to be there for you. The situation between your mother and I was an intense one. I had much love for her, but I had no intentions of leaving my home. Every time I look at you, I see her and it makes me remember the good times. I'm sorry I wasn't there for you like I was for Ross." He said.

His words were poetic to her heart and she could feel where he was coming from.

"I understand what you are saying. The past is the past and it can't be erased. I'm going to do all that I can to help you and Ross. Whether you want to believe it or not, we are all that we have. We can work on building a relationship later." With those words said between them she walked back to the bathroom to bathe Ross.

It was decided that Ross was going to stay with Mikleah. She was doing her best to care for her, but she was not there mentally or physically. She had not spoken and hadn't eaten in several days. Kleah was at her wits end. Ross was killing herself slowly and she could not help her do that. She was sure she needed professional help, because her condition was out of her realm of expertise.

She was able to get Jeremiah to draw up the proper paperwork giving her power of attorney over Ross, because she was incapacitated and could not make sound decisions.

She was able to find an awesome facility that dealt with victims' losing loved ones. Todd and Mikleah went to the hospital and met with the staff, whom she would entrust the care of her sister to.

After the short introductions between them, they toured the facility to see the type of treatment Ross was going to receive. Mikleah was completely satisfied with the entire visit and was ready to sign the papers for her admittance.

The ride to take Ross to her new home was a bittersweet one. Kleah was depressed because she couldn't help her. When they arrived Ross' personal medical staff was there to greet them.

She made sure that she was securely in her room.

"Ross I'm sorry that I have to leave you here. God knows that this was my last resort, but I can't let you die on me. You and I are all that we have. I need you here with

me. Please, for me, heed what the doctor is trying to do for you. I will be here every day to check on you and each time I come, I hope you are progressing. I love you, Ross" She kissed her forehead and headed for the door to leave.

The Booking
Chapter 16

"Mr. Jenks, how do you plead to the charge of statutory rape?" The judge asked Michael as he stood before him. He inhaled and answered, "Not guilty your honor."

"Judge Baker, my client has been falsely accused of this ludicrous charge. Michael Jenks has never been in any legal trouble. My client has been a law abiding citizen. I ask the court to take into consideration that Mr. Jenks has suffered several family tragedies." Jeremiah argued on behalf of his client. The battle was on. There were two heavyweights in the courtroom-one fighting for Michael and one fighting to lock his black ass up.

Angela Martinez, who was the lead attorney for the DA's office was a pit-bull in a skirt and was ready for war.

"Judge, Mr. Jenks has been accused of statutory rape of a 16-year old child. The evidence we have will satisfy the court's policy of guilty or innocence and prove him guilty as charged. I recommend that the defendant have a high bail. Being, that Mr. Jenks is a well-known community figure and has access to substantial monetary funds he may be a flight risk at best. Is this the type of man

you want to release out on bail your honor? Yes, it is true that he is experiencing family tragedies, but that is irrelevant to this proceeding. I ask that you look at the charges and not the defendant's current family situation."
She barked back just as forcefully as her opponent.

Michael stood listening to all the bullshit. He was not going anywhere. His wife was in the hospital and he just had a daughter committed into a mental facility. He had shit to do right in his own back yard. Michael was a lot of things, but one of them was not a deserter.

"Judge Baker my client is not going anywhere! The prosecution has no collaborating witnesses to this crime and there is no evidence that there has been a crime committed." Jeremiah said.

Judge Baker listened to both sides intently weighing each argument. He was quite aware that the defendant had been involved with a family scandal and his heart went out to him and his family. He wasn't there to judge Michael and whether or not he did the crime or not, he was only there to rule on his bail.

"Ladies and gentlemen in light of the evidence presented and the articulated arguments of both the defense and prosecution, I'm inclined to agree with both parties. It is true that the defendant has never been convicted of a

crime; but, today Mr. Jenks has been accused of a sex crime against a minor and this is a serious offense. Because of the type of charge that has been brought against him, I must set your bail on the high end at $500 thousand dollars. Next case Please!" That was that. Michael was on his way to lock up.

The bailiff came and placed the cold handcuffs on Michael. Before he was led out of the courtroom, Jeremiah told Michael to keep quiet, not talk to anyone, and that he would be down there as soon as possible.

Michael was stunned at the outcome of his bail hearing. He could not believe that his bail was half a million dollars. Since the time he started fucking, he had the hardest time telling his dick the word no. His mother had always warned him not to be like his father, but he never listened.

When Michael was 13 years old, his father's womanizing got him shot. His father was married to his mother but never could be faithful. Every time his mother caught him, his father would beg and plead for forgiveness and she would take him back.

The next affair that his father had was his last. His father began sleeping with another man's wife. One day while his mistress' old man was at work, Michael's father and his mistress were at play. They were so much at play that neither one of them heard the click of the loaded gun. The man aimed and shot Michael Sr. in the chest.

Although, Michael Sr. lived he was always reminded of how his dick had gotten him hemmed up, because a piece of the bullet remained in his chest as a constant reminder of how one choice had changed his entire life.

The trip downtown was finally over and Michael walked off the bus with the other inmates. He had never been in trouble so he had no idea what to expect. He had seen plenty of movies where suspects were booked, but that shit was just that, a movie and not reality. Once inside, he was finger printed and asked questions ranging from what tattoos he had to his sexual preference.

His mug shot was taken after giving the Corrections Officer his medical history. Afterwards, the humiliation really sat in. Michael was asked to strip butt ass naked in front of another man. Michael was reluctant at first, but when threatened, he quickly snapped out of his trance and complied. At that moment, he wished he was the one laying in the hospital and not his wife.

His day was long but he was relived to actually see his cell. It was good that he was not claustrophobic, because his jail cell was no bigger than a bedroom closet. He was locked up and he had no idea when he would make bail. Michael knew that he had to call Mikleah, because she was the only one who he could count on to handle his business and get him out.

The Weight of the World-Mikleah
Chapter 17

It had been a rough week and Mikleah was feeling down for the count. She wanted to call Todd and have him come to the house to light one up with her, but she knew she had to keep a clear head. She had to commit her sister to a mental facility and now the man who she just found out was her father was now facing a jail sentence. The shit was getting hectic.

She wanted to vent and get her frustration off her chest; the only person who she wanted to talk to was Jeremiah. She had his number programmed in her cell and decided to place a call to him. She was even more excited when he said that he'd come over after he got off work.

When he came to the house, they talked, and talked for what seemed like hours. When she was with him, Mikleah felt shielded from the outside world. Jeremiah stayed with her and held her in his arms until the morning light. She felt as if she was meant to be in his arms and she never wanted him to leave.

The next day she was able to finish making funeral arrangements for Lena, but was skeptical of what kind it would be; being that all of her immediate family was missing in action. It was time to go see Roses. She needed to be aware of what was going on.

Mikleah, called Dr. Muhammad to see if she was well enough for visitors. Because, her immediate family was nonexistent at the time, he made an exception for her. Jeremiah suggested she hold off on having the funeral until after going to see her.

Mikleah was terrified at the fact that she was going to see her mother's ex-lover in the hospital. She had done nothing wrong to her personally, but she still had resentment for her, because she rejected her mother. Kleah needed to look passed her petty thoughts and face her. She needed to know what was going on with her family.

Since Lena's death and Michael's arrest were still hot local stories, she was prepared to disguise herself before going to the hospital. The media was camping out at the hospital waiting to pounce on anyone they suspected had something to do with the story.

Jeremiah asked Mikleah if she wanted him to accompany her to tell Roses, but she told him it was a battle she needed to fight alone. Dr. Muhammad allowed her to see Roses after visiting hours the day before she was going to see Michael.

Mikleah's disguise for the outing was a blonde wig, a pantsuit, and Channel shades. She wore no make-up and *her attitude was funky-so if any nosy ass reporter was trying to get in her business they were going to have it. She decided not to drive herself. She called a limo service to drive her.*

For some reason, she was feeling more and more like her mother was so close that she could touch her. She told herself that her mother was with her in spirit always and she would be there guiding her when she needed her. Mikleah was ready for war!!!

When she arrived at the hospital, she was greeted by Dr. Muhammad.

"Welcome Mikleah I'm pleased to finally meet you. I feel like I already know you from all of our conversations." He said as they shook hands.

"No, doctor the pleasure is all mines. I'm just glad that you have allowed me to see Roses." She said.

Before going to the room, he explained Roses' current medical condition.

"I'm aware that you are not related to Ms. Jenks, but I will make an exception, because I am aware of the family situation. Let me start by saying, she has been making great progress. Roses came out of her coma on the same day of her mother's passing, but she suffered a mental breakdown when she learned of her mother's

death." He paused to make sure Mikleah was taking his words in.

"Wait, how does she know?" Kleah asked.

"Well, Roses woke up around the same time that the story about her mother was being broadcast. Once we made sure that she was fine, she was left in the room for less than 10 minutes. We were unaware of the breaking news and her television was on. She learned of the death from the breaking news. You see, although, Roses was in a coma, her brain was still functioning and processing. When she heard the news, it sent her into a mental breakdown." He said.

They sat and talked for another 20 minutes or so as he explained that she was better, but she had been prescribed Xanax for her anxiety. Mikleah could tell from the way he spoke of Roses that he took more of an interest in her besides being her physician. She looked at his left hand just to make sure he wasn't already some other woman's property.

Dr. Muhammad walked her to Roses' room and said, "She's yours. Just remember she's been through a lot and what you are coming to tell her is not the best of news." She took heed to his words, took a deep breath, and entered the dragon's den.

Locked up and They Won't Let me Out-Michael
Chapter 18

It had been a week and the money for bail still hadn't been raised. Michael had been living in a hell hole and his attorney and daughter were taking too damn long to get him out. Jeremiah was coming to see him. Mike hoped that he had some news on when he would get out.

He was able to get another bail hearing with a new judge. He was hoping and praying for a different result, at least a lower bail amount. Shit, he even knew that coming up with a half a million dollars was going to take a minute.

Since the time he got locked up, his days had been short and the nights had been long. He had been maintaining but this shit here was not for him. The niggas in jail hadn't tried him yet, but, he was preparing for when the shit popped off. The highlight of his day was meeting with Jeremiah. He was hoping that the meeting would produce good news.

"Jenks your lawyer is here." The CO yelled as he opened the steel doors and cuffed Mike in preparation to take him to his visit. He was led to an empty attorney room where he waited for Jeremiah.

Since, he was locked up, he had been unable to call the hospital to check on Roses. He made a mental note to have Jeremiah check on her. It's true what they say about jail. You have nothing but time to think.

All of his thoughts were on how he fucked up a perfectly good marriage by bringing a psychotic ass bitch in their lives. If his choices would have been different, then he would only have one daughter and his wife wouldn't have been turned out.

When Jeremiah walked in he could tell that something wasn't right. He sat in front of Michael and they exchanged pleasantries. After they greeted each other their conference began.

"Look Michael it is taking a little longer to get this $500k together but the money is getting there. What I need from you is your side of the story. Angela has some damning evidence that she assures will convict. She is offering a plea deal of one to two years with five years probation after your release. For some reason she is not offering a hard deal, it seems more like this deal is to teach a lesson of some sort." Jeremiah said as he opened his briefcase and took out Michael's legal documents.

Michael heard each word and snickered. He knew that Jade was behind all of this bullshit. It was true that he had fucked his boss' daughter and wife but that shit was over between them.

"Jeremiah, I don't know where to start this story, but I know who it ends with. Jade is pulling strings even from the grave!" Michael said.

Jeremiah had no idea who Jade was or the story behind her, but his gut told him that she was the key to his case in defending Mike.

"Start from the beginning and don't leave any stone unturned. If you want me to help you, I need to know what I'm dealing with." Little did he know he was about to take a journey into a wild and twisted story that he had no clue about. He took off his suit jacket, lit a Newport, and got comfortable for the story he was about to hear.

Mike met with Jeremiah for over two hours and he bared his soul to him. He told him everything. He felt better after their meeting and they decided that he would take the plea and serve the year in prison.

When Jeremiah showed him the evidence, there was no way he was going to beat the charges. He just knew once he got out; he would find out how in the hell Jade could have fucked him. He was saving his fire for when he was going to get out. Mike was going back to court to plead guilty to consensual sex with a minor and receive his sentence.

The Comfort of a Woman
Chapter 20

Mikleah walked into Roses' room and stood in the doorway before going to her bed. Her nerves were shot. She had to do this and there was no turning back now. She took a few deep breaths and walked over to where she was laying.

"Hello Roses, How are you feeling?" She asked as she sat in the chair next to her bed.

Roses turned and looked at her and said, "I'm doing well under the circumstances. I have been waiting for your visit. But where is my daughter, Mikleah?"Kleah's heart dropped. She had no idea where to start.

The whole family dilemma was fucked. How was she going to tell her that her daughter was in a mental institution and her husband was being accused of having sex with a minor?

"Roses there is a lot that I need to tell you and starting is not easy." Mikleah said as she stood and walked over to the window.

Silence filled the room. When she turned around, Roses was out of the bed. She looked weak but well rested. Roses had lost at least 20 pounds, but she was still as fine as ever. *She could see how her mother wanted her for herself.*

"*Mikleah lets go for a walk. I need some fresh air. I can tell that what you have to tell me is putting a strain on you. The fresh air will do us both good.*" Roses said.

She was relieved to see that Roses was somewhat in a good mood. They walked toward the terrace where there were seats available. As they walked, they had small talk but they both knew the conversation would soon turn serious.

They sat and stared at the shining stars in the sky.

"*God, I never knew how I took your magnificent works for granted.*" Roses said. *They both looked at the stars, while waiting for the other to get down to the business at hand.*

"*Roses, look since you have been in a coma so much has transpired. I'm sorry that I have to be the one filling you in. Dr. Muhammad informed me that you found out about Lena's death soon after waking up.*" Mikleah began.

Roses stared off in the distance and Mikleah could tell she was still grieving. "*Yeah, I woke up right around the time she killed herself. The news of her death is what sent me into a mantel state of shock.*" She said.

"*Mikleah, I'm not judging you,but learn from all of this twisted shit. Be smart about what you do, because all that you do will eventually come back to haunt you. There are many things, I wish I could change. I have many regrets.*" *Her eyes showed true remorse and sorrow.*

Kleah could tell she was looking for her soul's redemption. "*Thanks for the advice Roses. Your words have not fallen on deaf ears.*" *She told her.*

"*There is still more that you need to know. You see, Ross, Michael, and I were in the courtroom when Lena pulled the trigger. Ross lost it when she saw her grandma fall to her death. Since her passing, she hasn't been the same.*" *She was trying to tell her in a way that wouldn't shock her.*

"*Mikleah I know that you are trying to spare my feelings here, but I need to hear the unadulterated truth. All I ask is that you keep it real with me. Whatever it is you are here to tell me I will get through it.*" *Roses said.*

"*Roses, look no disrespect but look where we are! In a hospital! You are in a fragile condition and I'm not trying to have you relapse!*" *Kleah was trying to show tact and empathy and here she was asking for her to keep it real.....this was not how this conversation was supposed to go down.*

The tension between them was undeniable. In their silence, she reached for her hand and held it. Her touch was a touch that Mikleah longed for, a woman's touch. It was as if they read each other's mind because their eyes instantaneously connected and their lips interlocked in a passionate kiss.

In Kleah's mind, she was thinking what in the hell I'm I doing. The heat from between her inner lips were saying something totally different.

Mikleah's hands found Roses' secret valley. Her finger found its way to her moist waterfall and she was so tight that she came on herself from the excitement and anticipation. Roses sucked her nipples and they found themselves on the concrete getting it on.

Roses climbed on top of Kleah's face and lifted her garment. As she looked at her pussy, she was amazed at how perfectly shaved it was. Kleah didn't want to just eat her; she wanted to tease her too. Her thumb and forefinger went to work on her clit and on the inside of her tight pussy.

Roses was in heaven from her touch. She tilted her head upwards and started grabbing and sucking her nipples. They turned into the 69 position and pleased each other. They were so in-tuned with each other's bodies that they climaxed at the same time.

After their intimate encounter, Roses laid in her arms. They relished in the moment because they both knew that this would never happen again.

The moment that they shared was one of consolation. As the stars shined down on their bodies and the southern night's air was breezy, Mikleah was able to find her voice and finish what she set out to do; which was to tell Roses everything.

"Roses, I know that your tension is gone from your body, because mine sure is." Mikleah said as they both laughed at the comment.

"I really want to finish telling you what's going." She said as she looked at Roses.

"Mikleah, laying here in your arms brings me back to when I was with your mother. You remind me so much of her. Please... just hold me...just for tonight and tomorrow we can finish this conversation." She did as she was told and they lied under the stars until the morning light.

It was five in the morning when they awoke and hurried back to the hospital room before the medical staff could realize she was gone all night. They made it back to the room just before the new shift started. Kleah sat in the chair next to the bed and closed her eyes.

Her mind saw visions of Jeremiah. It was like he was reaching out for her and she didn't want to let him go. She went out the room and called him from her cell.

"Good morning." She said as chipper as she could into the phone.

"Well how are you sexy lady? I dreamed of you last night and wanted you next to me. How are you doing?" His deep and sexy voice echoed through the phone.

"I'm so much better now that I have heard your voice. I just wanted to call you because you were on my mind and to thank you for the other night. You were there for me and gave me a shoulder to lean on. So thank you." She told him.

"Mikleah, you know that I'm feeling you and you are feeling me, so spending any time with you is my pleasure. Yes, I'm glad to hear your voice this morning. My day is going to be a good one thanks to you, but baby I have to go, I have an early start today. Call me tonight when you are free and perhaps we can get together for dinner." Jeremiah said.

Her heart skipped a beat when he said he was feeling her. "I will think about calling you later but you have a great day and think about me!" She said hanging up not giving him an opportunity to respond.

After hearing Jeremiah's voice, she was ready to face the world. She had pushed the night before out of her mind and was focusing on what was ahead of her with Roses.

Mikleah walked back into the room and noticed Roses had drifted off to sleep. She turned the television on and watched a few minutes of the news before the television was watching her. She was awakened by a knock on the door. Before, she could see who was at the door she saw Dr. Muhammad walking in. "Good morning doctor." She said as she wiped the sleep from her eyes and searched her purse for a mint.

"Well good morning to you too! I see that you have made yourself at home. I hope that the two of you enjoyed your evening." He said as he walked over to the bed. Roses and Mikleah looked at each other with smirks thinking about what they had done.

Glancing at her watch, Kleah realized that it was a quarter to 12 and she needed to run errands.

"Roses and Dr. Muhammad I must be leaving. I didn't realize how late it was." She said as she got up to leave.

"Um, no you don't Mikleah!!! We haven't finished talking and you can not leave until I know what's going

on!" Roses responded as she looked her in her eyes.

"Roses don't you want me to come back after Dr. Muhammad is done examining you?" Was all Mikleah could say.   "No! Whatever you need to say to me, you can say in front of the man who has been caring for me the last few months!!! You can start by telling me when and where my mother's funeral is?" Her eyes darted from Mikleahs's into Dr. Muhammad eyes.

"First of all, I decided to hold off on the time and place until I had spoken with you. Her body is at Flowers, James and Johnson Funeral Home and all of the expenses have been paid. The only thing for you to do is decide when and where." In her mind the battle was half done. The only the situation left was with Ross and Michael.

"Mikleah thank you for making the arrangements but why didn't Michael handle it? He would have known exactly what momma would have wanted." She asked.

Her questions made her stomach churn. She knew it was coming to this. Of course she was going to want to know where the hell her husband was. She looked at Dr. Muhammad and searched his face for a sign as to how to tell her. His face was just as blank as hers.

"Roses, Michael is fine. He just hasn't been able to come and see you yet." These were all the words she could

muster.   *"Mikleah if you don't tell me what in the hell is going on; I will get up and beat your ass like you were a runaway slave and I was your master!!!" Her voice was extremely loud, clear, and to the point.*

"There's no need for threats of bodily harm. At least, let her tell you what see needs to tell you." Dr. Muhammad said as he looked at her with a look that said you better calm down- I want to hear this shit.

"I apologize Mikleah. I just want to know what's up. Please understand where I'm coming from." She said.

"It's cool. I understand. I want to be careful about my choice of words. Look Roses this is what's going on. The day your mother died, Michael was served with legal papers." She didn't want to tell her all at once but in sections until she knew everything.

"What kind of papers? What are you talking about?" Roses asked as she looked at Dr. Muhammad for him to make sense of what she was hearing. Mikleah swallowed hard, closed her eyes, and said a silent prayer. She started the story again.

"As the three of us were being escorted from the courtroom, a woman came from out of nowhere and served Michael, saying that she was representing some family. She said that he was being charged with statutory rape of a

minor." It came out so fast that she was sure that Roses missed what was said. But Roses was on it and didn't miss a beat.

"What! Charged with statutory rape! The rape of who Mikleah?" Her voice carried into the hallway and some nosy nurses started to turn their heads to see what was going on. She got up and closed the door so the conversation could stay as private as possible.

"Who's accusing him? Roses asked.

"I have no idea who would do this." Kleah said as she answered her question.

"Where is he Mikleah? Who's representing him and where is Rosslyn?" Roses' mind was going at 100 miles per hour. She had so many questions going through her head that needed to be answered. Roses was hoping for the best but preparing for the worst.

"Roses, the same attorney that was representing your mother before her death is now representing Michael. You know he is one of the best attorneys in the state. He is doing all he can for Michael. There was a slight set back we didn't anticipate his bail to be so high." She said.

"So what are you saying Mikleah! What the fuck are you saying to me?!!!"Roses shouted.

Mikleah looked at Roses and opened her mouth.

When she did these words came out, "Roses, both Rosslyn and Michael are locked up. Ross is in a mental institution and Michael is in jail!"

The last words that Mikleah heard Roses say were:

"What, What…. What the Fuck!!!"

www.ingramcontent.com/pod-product-compliance
Lightning Source LLC
Chambersburg PA
CBHW070846120626
46556CB00002B/904